"I BOUGHT YOU SOMETHING. . . ."

Hunter handed Amelia a small leather box. She gasped in pleased surprise and threw her arms around his neck.

"You haven't even opened it!" He laughed uncomfortably and struggled gently to free himself.

"Anything from you I will love. You thought of me! You are the dearest man alive." She released him and hugged her arms around herself instead. Her insides hurt from loving him so much.

"It is a betrothal present."

It was just like him to be so thoughtful. How silly that he should be so shy about giving it to her. He had gone over to stare out the window at the passing traffic. She opened the box. In the little, white silk coffin lay a set of sapphire earrings and a pendant of the same stone. "Hunter . . ." She was unable to say more.

"I thought they would match your eyes."

Her head jerked up in surprise. "But my eyes are green."

"Are they?" Hunter crossed the room to look at her with interest. "So they are. I suppose they look blue sometimes."

"Really?" Pressing back a feeling of disappointment, she smiled brightly. "They are lovely. I will wear them tonight."

THE HERO RETURNS

Catherine Blair

ZEBRA BOOKS
Kensington Publishing Corp.
http://www.zebrabooks.com

ZEBRA BOOKS are published by

Kensington Publishing Corp.
850 Third Avenue
New York, NY 10022

First Printing: December, 1999
10 9 8 7 6 5 4 3 2 1

Printed in the United States of America

One

"He's here!" Amelia's voice was very near an ungenteel screech. She leapt up from the seat by the window that she had occupied for the better part of an hour.

"Amelia, don't. . . ." her sister protested, putting down her needlework with an exasperated sigh. "You are practically screaming. Endeavor to show Westhaven that you have grown into *something* of a lady." But the bang of the door was accompanied by a wild shriek in the hallway, and Miriam had to be content with pressing her fingers to her temples and wincing.

Amelia's slippers skidded on the polished marble floor of the hall, and she nearly collided with the butler. He obviously also had been watching for the arrival. "He's here!" she repeated jubilantly. Harrison smiled indulgently and opened the door. She slipped out the instant it was open wide enough and catapulted down the steps to fling herself into the arms of a tall gentleman barely dismounted from his horse.

"Oh, Hunter! You're back! I thought you would never be back soon enough! I thought every day that I would die without you!" She pressed her face into the shoulder of his coat and inhaled deeply. He smelled just as she remembered: wool and starch and something else that was only Hunter. He was here, really here after three agonizingly long years. She released him enough to pull back and look up at his face. Involuntarily, she drew a quick breath. He was so very changed! His face still had the familiar handsome lines, but he was brown from the sun and perhaps thinner than before. The Spanish sun also had lightened his dark hair slightly, and somehow this made his brown eyes appear an almost pupil-less black. His mouth, always ready to laugh before, seemed set in a straight line. There was a new tenseness about his features.

"Hello, Millie. I see that you recognize me," he said calmly, the edge of irony in his voice showing that he had not missed her reaction to the changes in him. He detached her arms from around his neck and held her back to inspect her. "You are looking well." He smiled, but the act seemed unnatural for him and did not reach his eyes.

She again pressed her face into his shoulder. "I read all the published dispatches. You were mentioned so honorably. I was so proud—"

"Ah, so the hero has returned!" a voice boomed.

"Jack!" Hunter removed Amelia gently from his person and stepped over to shake hands with her older brother, who had come out of the house accompanied by Miriam and Lady Harrow. "You are looking fit. In fact, you are all blooming." He greeted her family cordially, and they all went inside. Amelia followed, dogging his footsteps as she had since she was eight years old.

"It was good of you to ride over to see us so soon, Lord Westhaven. You must have arrived at Crownhaven only last night. Your mother surely could not wish to give you up to the neighbors just yet. How sorry Lord Harrow will be to have missed you. He has gone up to Town for the week." Lady Harrow gave Harrison instructions for tea and then settled herself in a crimson upholstered chair. Amelia sat down on the small couch and looked up at Hunter. The painful surge of joy she felt seemed to have left no room in her body for her heart. It was awkwardly crushed within her chest.

He seated himself beside her and clasped his hands firmly in his lap. "How could I refuse such a kind invitation from Miss Harrow?"

"Amelia! You did not write to Lord Westhaven, did you? How terribly rude. You should at least have let him catch his breath! I would not be surprised if you demanded that he come see you instantly."

"Enough, Miriam," Lady Harrow murmured.

Amelia narrowed her eyes at her sister and then returned her full gaze to Hunter. "I can't believe you are really here," she repeated.

He gave a short laugh. "I can't believe it myself. It is very strange to think that even while I sit here taking tea with you in your beautiful, peaceful home, there is a war raging and men dying of wounds, infection, and disease on the Peninsula." His mouth tightened. "But that is not a topic for mixed company. Pray forgive me. I am fortunate to be able to come home to such a loving family and kind neighbors."

"Does your wound pain you very much?" Amelia asked, touching him very gently on the arm. "I thought I would go mad with fear for you when I heard that you had been hurt."

"I still have very little strength in that arm. Today was the first time I tried to ride. It was a bit of a challenge, even with an animal as well-trained as my roan. I daresay I will regain most of my movement and strength in time. I would rather have stayed with my regiment, but I would have been of little use to them." He shrugged carelessly, but there was a hard expression in his eyes. "There was very little cause for you to worry. I told you that every time that I wrote."

"But you hardly ever wrote," Amelia replied reprovingly, giving him a coquettish look from beneath her lashes. But it was unkind to take him to task for such things. It hardly mattered now; he was home.

Hunter seemed at a loss as to how to respond and smiled tensely in relief when the tea tray arrived.

"You have laid off wearing your regimentals, Major," Jack stated indignantly.

"Well, I have sold my commission now because of the wound—"

"Nonsense, you should keep wearing the scarlets. You know how the petticoat set loves them." He gave Hunter a broad wink.

"Jack, how can you say such a thing!" Amelia protested. "I think Hunter looks fine in anything he wears."

"Thank you, Millie. I knew I could count on you to come to my defense."

Jack shrugged easily and abandoned the subject. "So tell us, Major, how long before we whip the Frenchies?" he asked, stacking a colossal number of tea cakes onto his plate.

Westhaven sighed. He suddenly looked a good deal older than his twenty-nine years. "It cannot continue like this for long. The losses on both sides are so crippling. . . . I don't see how it can go on." He seemed to come to himself in a snap. "But of course England will prevail. There is no doubt about that."

"Just so!" Jack exclaimed. "I wanted so much to go myself. But of course Father said no. Only son and all that." He stretched out his long nankeen-clad legs and examined the shine of his tasseled hessians.

"Of course," Westhaven echoed, unable to look at him.

"How are your mother and brother?" Miriam asked.

"They are fine, thank you. I was pleased to find how well Thomas has managed the estate. I always tell him that we should have switched places at birth, and he should have been the eldest and taken the title and Crownhaven, while I should have been the dissolute younger brother, fit only for soldiering."

"Yes, I remember how upset your father was when you joined the dragoons," Lady Harrow remarked. There was a silence while everyone recalled the late Lord Westhaven. He had died over a year ago, but his son had not come home for the funeral.

"He was determined not to have his heir risk his health"—he gave a hard laugh at his own choice of words—"for something so bourgeois as Britain's freedom. As far as he was concerned, I should have lived out my life in a glass display case while Thomas joined the military or the church or whatever it is that second sons are forced to take up, regardless of their inclination. I'm half surprised he didn't cut me out in favor of my brother as his heir when he discovered that I had joined."

"You were right to go," Amelia said firmly. "Our country needs more men like you to lead our soldiers." She was rewarded with a slight smile from Hunter and a pat on the hand.

"Perhaps, Amelia"—Lady Harrow set down her teacup, "you would like to show Lord Westhaven the garden. We have worked very hard to change it into a Wild Garden. They are all the rage, you know. I fancy we have made quite a few improvements since you used to run tame here years ago." She smiled archly at the couple and stood to show them to the door.

"What a pleasant idea," Hunter replied with grace.

Amelia took his arm and led him through to the back of the house. It was nice to feel him so close beside her at last. He was taller than she remembered. Though she herself was taller than her older sister and reckoned quite the long meg, she only came up to his chin. She looked at the strong profile of his chin and mouth and suddenly felt tongue-tied. How silly. He had been a part of her life forever. Ever since she was a child, she had adored him. But now he seemed a different man.

"We cut down the old maze and have put in succession houses," she said, gesturing. "I knew you would have been sorry to see the maze go. We used to have such fun in there. Do you remember the time that Thomas jumped out at Miriam, and she ran around and around screaming and could not get out? She was such a goose because of course we all knew the way out very well. I went in there just before they cut it down and could still do every turn blindfolded." They walked for a few moments in silence, stopping to admire the profusion of early summer blooms artfully arranged in clusters for the maximum uncultivated effect.

"Miriam is staying with us while her husband is in Jamaica. He has a sugarcane plantation there or some such thing. You do remember that she married Lord Wells last winter? She could not accompany him as she is . . . in a family way." She felt a blush rising up her neck and tried to swallow it back down. "We put in a new sundial and took out the bed with the columbines and lobelia. I wanted to try a water garden, but Mama and Miriam said that it would be the height of pretension. So we have put in this trellis and the bench instead."

She led him to the bench and suggested that they sit for a moment. She instantly wished that she hadn't, for now it seemed that they must speak personally. Three years suddenly seemed like a very long time indeed. They sat in silence for a few moments, and Amelia tried to remember not to fidget.

"It is nice to see you again, Millie," Hunter began after clearing his throat. "You have grown up."

"Miriam would argue with you about that," she replied with a rueful laugh. "Though I am past twenty and quite an old maid. I shouldn't have thrown myself at you so hoydenishly when you arrived." The painful joy she had experienced at his arrival had subsided to a dull, anxious ache. She could not bring herself to look at him.

"Not at all," he said gallantly, "I quite enjoyed it." Several birds in the trees by the succession houses began a noisy quarrel. They both watched them for a few moments in silence.

"Hunter," she said at last, when she could stand the tension no more, "are we still betrothed?"

There was a painful, long silence during which Amelia began to feel extremely ill.

"Do you wish to be?" he asked quietly at last.

"Yes, yes, I do. Very much." She turned her face anxiously up to his. He was looking at her, but his dark eyes were entirely unreadable. "I wrote to you every week. You know how I love you. You know I have been waiting for you all this time." She stopped the flow of words by biting her lower lip. "But perhaps you would wish me to release you from the engagement," she said, forcing the tremor out of her voice.

This time the pause was almost infinitesimal. "Of course not. We shall be married very soon. I would be very honored."

Amelia realized that the blood pounding in her ears had become a deafening ring and released her breath. Pulling him to his feet, she flung her arms around his neck and clung tightly to him. "Oh, Hunter, I am so happy. I am even happier now than when you first asked me. Because now you are back, and we can be married soon!" She released him and danced lightly in front of him, holding his hands. He smiled indulgently down at her.

"Can it be *very* soon?" she asked.

"Whenever you like."

"In London? Could we please be married in London? In St. George's? Will you put the announcement in the paper right away? Mama will be so pleased that you still want to marry me. She counseled me not to expect it, even though we did pledge ourselves before you left. Oh, I am beyond everything happy!"

"We can do whatever you wish," Westhaven repeated.

"Aren't you happy?" Amelia's brows drew together.

"Of course, Millie. Of course I am happy. I am just overwhelmed with my good fortune. Besides, you have always had more energy than me. Even when you were a girl."

"Oh, Hunter, I would have followed you anywhere then. And you know I still would. I always dreamed of the day when we would be married. You were my hero. Of course now you are everyone's hero!" She laughed delightedly. "I have kept everything the papers have ever published about you and your regiment. Oh, three years was such a long time. I thought it would never end, but now it has and now everything will be good because you are home, and we can start our lives again."

Westhaven looked down at the pretty, pixie-like face of his betrothed. Her dark curls were dressed in the most fashionable of styles and her gown was surely straight from the pages of *Ackermann's Repository*, but there was still something childish, almost worshipful, in her open expression of trust. He felt a wave of something like pity. It surprised him, as it was the first emotion he had felt since he had left Spain. "Yes, Millie," he said woodenly, "we can start our lives again."

Two

Amelia was awakened early by the growling rumble of thunder. She shifted in bed, opened her eyes, and squinted in the bright sunlight. The low thundering sound continued, and she now realized that it was comprised of the hoofbeats and carriage wheels synonymous with city traffic. She had been three days in London, but the terrific noise of the metropolis was still surprising to her.

Cuddling deeper into the bedding, she examined the room around her with a satisfied sigh. It was fashionably furnished in peacock blue and gold, and the paint had barely been dry when she arrived. But she should not grow too fond of it. Soon she would move into Hunter's town house as his wife.

Yes, everything would be perfect from now on. The past three years had been agonizing. She had spent most of her time at home or going on long solitary rides, while the rest of her friends had had their London season. They had gone on to make matches of varying degrees of brilliance, while she wrote letters to Spain. For three years, her life had hung in the balance, depending on a general's decisions and French marksmanship. But now everything would be different.

She ran lightly down the stairs, pulling on her dressing gown as she went. "Walker?" she called out. Rather than ring for him, she continued down the servant stairs to the kitchen. The town house butler looked up in surprise from where he was ironing the newspaper.

"Miss Harrow!" he exclaimed, looking about behind him for his coat. Unable to locate it immediately, he crossed his arms, as if to hide the nakedness of his exposed shirtsleeves.

"Is that the *Times*, Walker?" Amelia pounced upon it eagerly.

"Why, yes. But I have not finished with it yet, miss."

"Yes, yes, I just wanted to see something."

"Is your announcement coming out today, Miss Amelia?" Cook grinned and wiped her hands on her apron. "I could see by the shining light in your eyes that today was the day of your announcement. Do read it aloud for all of us." The woman helped Walker find the armhole of his coat and patted his lapels down soothingly. He was visibly ruffled by the shirtsleeve incident.

"Here it is! Miss Amelia Harrow, daughter of Baron Clement Harrow and Lady Sofia Harrow of Harrow End, Bedfordshire, will wed Viscount John Hunter Kirby Westhaven, Major lately of His Majesty's 12th Dragoon Regiment."

"And?" Cook prompted.

"Well, that is all. We have not had a chance to fix a date yet. I think July." Amelia gave a skip. "I must go and show this to Miriam. Don't bother about it not being pressed, Walker. I won't let it smudge anything." She waved the paper cheerfully in response to the butler's pained expression and ran back up the stairs.

"Miriam!" She burst breathlessly into her elder sister's room. "See what is in the paper today!"

"Amelia, you would think that you are the first girl on earth to get engaged," a voice croaked from the bed.

"Oh, but you don't understand. I have been waiting for this for so long."

"I know." Miriam sat up, cast off her nightcap, and made room for her in the bed. "Now don't bounce. You will make me ill, and I am just over feeling ill every minute until after lunch.

"Very nice," she continued, looking dutifully over the announcement. "I am very happy for you, Millie, because I know you have waited for Hunter for such a long time. However, I must say, you have spent so much time and energy worrying over him—"

"But it is all worth it now." Amelia smiled blissfully. She leaned back and gazed at the stars embroidered on the canopy over the bed, remembering the feel of Hunter's arms around her.

"Yes . . ." her sister replied hesitantly, "but it has been such a long time since you have been in each other's company. You were but seventeen when he left. He has gone through so much. It must have changed him. He is not the same boy who used to play with us when we were children. He hardly seems the same man who left three years ago. He seems a good deal older than thirty."

"He is nine-and-twenty."

Miriam gave her an infuriatingly indulgent smile. "And of course you have changed, too. Perhaps it would have been better to wait a while to see if you still suit before announcing the betrothal."

"But Hunter and I don't want to wait!" Amelia protested. "I know we have changed, but I wrote him all the time, and he wrote me when he could. . . . We still love each other, and how could we wait longer when we have waited so long already?" She knew that her sister was only trying to be rational, but there was no way that anyone could understand how desperately she needed Hunter, especially now that he was back.

Miriam must have seen the expression on her face. "Don't mind me, dear," she said cheerfully. "You go on and dream your bride dreams and leave your crabby, old sister alone to sleep."

"To sleep, perchance to dream of your lovey-dovey husband in far-off Jamaica," she replied mockingly.

"I am asleep, Millie, and I cannot hear you," came the reply from beneath a pillow.

"Then you will not know that I am stealing your garnets to wear at the betrothal ball tonight," Amelia whispered in a comical sotto voce voice.

"I am not that asleep. Yes, yes, borrow them, Millie, but see that you don't lose them, you featherwit."

Amelia held out her arms from her sides and allowed herself to be dressed like a large doll. Her brows were drawn together slightly.

"You look very well, miss," her mother's maid said approvingly. "The claret trimmings make your skin look so very white."

"Thank you," she replied absently.

"The rubies are perfect, miss."

She hadn't needed to borrow the garnets after all. Hunter's mother had sent over a dazzling set of rubies that had belonged to Hunter's paternal grandmother. Her parents must have known about the intended betrothal gift, for they had presented her with a set of ruby and diamond brilliants for her hair.

"Thank you." Amelia took one last look in the chervil glass. She had so rarely attended balls that it was peculiar to see herself dressed for one. The white crepe overdress, embellished with claret-colored rouleau at the neck and hem, was open in the front to reveal an underdress of silver-shot silk. It was far more sophisticated than the plain gowns she was used to wearing. Her dark brown hair looked near black the way it was pulled into a knot at the top and dressed to fall in little curls around her oval face. She looked scared.

"Well!" she said stoutly, frowning at her reflection. "There is no use hiding up here any longer. Thank you for your help, Marie." She took her gloves and fan from the dressing table and started down the stairs.

She saw Hunter instantly, standing with her mother and his own mother at the foot of the stairs. The tenseness in her stomach became an uncomfortable twist of nervous joy. He looked up at her, the lights from the chandelier highlighting the planes of his face and the depth of his dark eyes. His face was blank. His reaction when he saw her was . . . was not a reaction at all. Wasn't he happy to see her? She saw his throat move as he swallowed.

"Hunter," she said, with a tremulous smile, "what is wrong? Don't you recognize me?" She held out both of her hands to him.

"I hardly did. You have grown up so much." He took her hands and bowed over them, his face still serious. Amelia wished that he would smile. It seemed like he had hardly done so since he had returned.

"Thank you so much for the betrothal gift, Lady Westhaven." She touched the ruby necklace at her throat. "You wrote in the note you sent with the set that they had been in the family for a long time."

"Indeed they have. Hunter's grandmama presented them to me on my betrothal. Though I was never overfond of them myself." She examined them through her lorgnette for a moment and then turned away. "You should begin to receive your guests, Lady Harrow."

Amelia's mother gave a slightly annoyed laugh. "You will of course join us in the receiving line, Lady Westhaven." Lady Harrow motioned to her husband and he reluctantly detached himself from a knot of his cronies and joined his wife in the receiving line. Amelia heard the orchestra tuning their instruments in the ballroom upstairs, and the first of the guests began to arrive. She turned to her fiancé and felt her stomach flutter.

"I feel very shy. I have never been the focus of so much attention before. I am glad that you are here with me."

He smiled at last, but it was brief and tight-lipped. "You always loved attention as a girl. I think we all supposed that you would run off to become an actress. There is nothing to fear tonight." He patted her hand, but there was something perfunctory about it. Amelia decided that he must be feeling nervous, too.

Her own shyness faded quickly, once the guests began arriving in earnest. It was so comforting to have Hunter at her side and to hear his strong voice replying so calmly to everyone's greetings. She resisted the temptation to lean her head against his shoulder, close her eyes, and just listen to him.

"Well, then," said her mother at last, "I think that most everyone has arrived. We should open the dancing."

Amelia agreed, wishing she could sit down for a few moments. Her cheeks felt stiff from smiling and making the proper replies to all of the wellwishers. She tried subtly to rub some feeling back into them.

Taking the hand he offered her, she allowed Hunter to lead her up to the ballroom. She had only danced with him a few times before he had left for Spain, but he performed the quadrille with perfect grace. Even without his regimental scarlet, there was something military in his carriage that emphasized his height and the broadness of his shoulders. He smiled his peculiar, sad, new smile at her.

"Did I tell you that you look very beautiful tonight?"

Amelia felt her cheeks grow warm with pleasure. "I—I think that you did." She raised her eyes to his. "But I love to hear it from you, Hunter." She knew then that she was perfectly content and that nothing could ever happen to make her either more or less happy. This was to be the beginning of a long, warm dream that would last the rest of her life.

The music ended, and she gave a delighted laugh as he bowed formally over her hand. They promenaded halfway around the room together and then he led her back to her mother

"Shall I get you some refreshment?"

"How kind of you to offer. No, thank you. I am quite happy as I am."

He stood by her until her next partner came to claim her for a country dance. She watched Hunter for as long as she could see him as he withdrew to the card room.

"I have never seen a girl so much in love," Mr. Bloome said, with a jovial laugh as he led her into the set that was forming.

"I cannot bear to let him out of my sight." Amelia laughed, too. "I was so long without him, that being apart for a minute now that he is back is very agonizing indeed." It was foolish for her to have hoped that he would remain in her presence the whole evening. Surely he would come back and dance again with her later in the evening, and of course he would take her in to eat after the supper dance.

"Your betrothed is a queer bird, Milz!" Jack announced bluntly as he escorted his sister in to supper.

"How dare you say that!"

"Well, I only mean that it is damned odd that he would not take his own fiancée in to supper. It *is* considered the done thing." He thought for a moment. "Especially at your own betrothal ball."

"I am certain that he is simply distracted and has lost track of the time," Amelia shot back. "He is most likely looking for me right now. Besides, you have known Hunter all of your life. You know as well as I that he is very well-mannered." Despite the difference in their sex, Jack was only two years older than herself, and she had always felt closer to him than Miriam. But of course this also gave her the liberty to think him the most chuckle-headed creature to walk the earth.

"Yes, the model of all perfections," her brother agreed with a roll of his eyes. "But he has been different since he came back. Closed-lipped, you know. Walks out in the middle of conversations. Doesn't want to go to mills or cockfights."

"Just because he doesn't want to take part in barbaric forms of amusement hardly means that there is something wrong with him!"

"No." Jack scratched his chin thoughtfully. "He just seems . . . restless. Johnston came back like that, too. Didn't enjoy anything. Dead bore." He haphazardly filled a plate with food and handed it to his sister.

"He has only been back a few weeks. It will take him some time to adjust. He will be just like the old Hunter in no time."

" 'Course." He bobbed his head with reassuring vigor. "In no time at all. Let's just hope he comes to his senses before he marries you, brat."

"Ha ha." She gave him a sour look which changed instantly to one of pleasure as she saw Hunter enter the dining room. "Look, there he is." She gestured triumphantly. "I told you that he did not forget me."

"Your knight in shining armor," Jack laughed. "Just be sure you don't put him on a pedestal too high. You might see that his feet are made of coal."

"What?"

"Isn't that what they say? That you shouldn't worship a god whose feet are made of coal?"

"I think you mean clay."

"Well, I never could abide all them Greeks anyway. Damn obscure stuff." He waved Hunter over and pulled out a chair for Amelia.

"It is from the Bible, goose! No wonder you were sent down from the university. Well, Hunter has lovely feet, and they definitely are not made of clay."

"He certainly does have nice boots," Jack conceded. "Are they Hoby? I must ask him."

"Please forgive me for being late, Amelia. I cannot see how I came to lose track of the time." Hunter bowed over her hand, and then turned to her brother. "What was it you wished to ask me?"

"Your boots. Hoby? I thought so. How do you contrive to give them that shine? Your man has some secret brought back from Spain, I fancy. Champagne? Bear fat? Perhaps he polishes them with French blood." Jack laughed boisterously.

"Hardly." Hunter's reply was repressive.

"Perhaps," Amelia said, with a peculiar, high laugh, "he uses clay."

Three

Hunter pulled on his boots and stood up from the bed. He wandered the room absently for a moment, as though he was looking for something, and then stopped at the window. There was nothing to see. The rain came down in perpendicular gray streams exactly as though there was a sieve of water above the window. It looked as if it would only get darker, though it was only five in the afternoon.

"That's it?" came a voice from the bed.

Hunter did not answer.

"You don't want anything else?"

"No." His throat felt dry. He didn't feel like talking. Perhaps he shouldn't have even come to see Angelina. She always wanted to talk.

"Come on, darling, once more. Put some feeling into it this time!" She laughed as though this was very funny.

"I can tell you're an actress."

"Well, I mean it." She got out of bed and followed him to the window, indifferent to the facts that she was naked and the drapes were open. "You bring me such nice presents and things, and then you don't want anything hardly. I mean, you could just get a girl for the night if you only wanted a quick tumble."

Hunter looked at her levelly for a moment. "Indeed." He turned away from the window and picked up his coat from a chair. "You are aware that I am to be married?"

"I suppose you said so," she replied, following him across the room. "If it don't bother you, it don't bother me," she gave him a broad wink and laughed.

He waited for her to stop. "Well, that's just it. It does. I shall not be needing your services in the future." He removed a bag, heavy with coins, from his coat pocket. "I assume you prefer this to a bankdraft?"

"What?" She looked insulted.

He eased himself into his coat, wincing over his wounded shoulder.

"But it hasn't been more than a month!" she protested when he didn't reply.

He shrugged and tossed the bag onto a table. He thought he saw her eyes brighten at the resounding thunk it made. "Nonetheless. I am resolved. Thank you so much for your time." He bowed over the hand of the naked woman, repressing a smirk at the ridiculousness of the gesture, and strode out of the room.

Once on the street, he drew a deep, relieved breath. The city stank in the summer; he had forgotten about that. But in the rain, the smell of sewage and horses and coal mingled with something nicer. It was not the smell of the country rain. It was more like that of water simmering on the warm pavement. Yes, it stank, but it was a good stink.

His mind snapped back to the smells of the battlefield—the hot, choking smell of gunpowder and sweat. God, how could it be that something so English as rain could drag his mind back to Spain? Three years of his life seemed doomed to haunt him forever. He pushed the thoughts away and turned up the collar of his coat. Of course he should have brought an umbrella, but it hadn't seemed important this morning.

As he made his way down Piccadilly, he realized that

he must have looked somewhat eccentric with his curly-brimmed beaver dripping rain and the lapels of his coat standing on end. Two dandies, one with a watch-fob only slightly smaller than his head, looked up from the absorbing task of maneuvering their white pantaloons around the muddy puddles to gasp in audible horror. Westhaven grinned and tipped his hat to them. A stream of water spouted forth from its rim.

He turned up Bond Street, even though he had no business there. Actually, he had no business anywhere. The idea of spending the day at his club overwhelmed him with a vague sense of anxiety. Spending the afternoon at the town house dancing attendance on his mother was no better. He was glad to be rid of Angelina. He had employed her simply because she was the most sought-after courtesan this season, but he found that having a mistress, *de rigueur* as it might be, did not suit him. She never gave him a moment's peace with her eternal chatter.

He examined the contents of the store windows with leisurely thoroughness, amusing himself by trying to recall what had changed since he was here before leaving for Spain. The apothecary was replaced by yet another tailor's establishment and the tobacco shop on the corner was under another name. There was very little that he actually recognized from before. Could it really have been three years?

He thought of Amelia and scowled. Her presence in his mind always induced a wrench of guilty annoyance. She was too good for him. Too damned cloying. He stumped through a deep puddle, heedless of its spoiling the gloss of his hessians. It was not the rain that was drowning him.

* * *

"I bought you something," Hunter announced with little ceremony. He handed Amelia a small leather box. She gasped in pleased surprise and threw her arms around his neck.

"You haven't even opened it!" He laughed uncomfortably and struggled gently to free himself.

"Anything from you I will love. You thought of me! You are the dearest man alive." She released him and hugged her arms around herself instead. Her insides absolutely hurt from loving him so much.

"It is a betrothal present."

It was just like him to be so thoughtful. How silly that he should be so shy about giving it to her. He had gone over to stare out the window at the passing traffic. She opened the box. In the little, white silk coffin lay a set of sapphire earrings and a pendant of the same stone. "Hunter . . ." She was unable to say more.

"I thought they would match your eyes."

Her head jerked up in surprise. "But my eyes are green."

"Are they?" Hunter crossed the room to look at her with interest. "So they are. I suppose they look blue sometimes."

"Really?" Pressing back a feeling of disappointment, she smiled brightly. "They are lovely. I will wear them tonight. You do remember that we are going to the theatre, don't you?"

"Yes, of course. How could I forget?"

She bit back a retort that seemed obvious. "Your mother and brother will come?"

"Yes."

"And tomorrow you will take me for a drive in the park like you promised?"

He hesitated. "If the weather is fair."

His smile was taut. He was getting the hunted look that she was becoming familiar with. She shut the jewelry case with a snap and dropped it onto the sofa. "Oh, Hunter darling, you must forgive me for clinging. You have been away for so long." She held both of her hands out to him. "I feel as though I can't bear to have you out of my sight." He took her hands, but his expression was inscrutably blank. "And I have not seen very much of you since you returned," she explained, a tone of pleading creeping into her voice. He did not reply, but looked distinctly uncomfortable.

"Oh, well," she continued brightly, "I suppose when we are married, I will see you a good deal more." But even as she said it, she was beginning to suspect that it would be very far from the fact.

When Lord Westhaven led her into the box at the Drury Lane Theatre, Amelia tried not to gape. The theatre was smaller than she had thought it would be, but it was so much more crowded. Affecting an expression of cool boredom, she raised her opera glasses and examined her surroundings. The ceiling was painted and gilt, but it was hard to see with the chandeliers blazing. She was glad that they had box seats, for she had heard that the candles often dripped hot wax on the patrons in the pit.

That region was crowded with people, mostly men dressed in clothes so fashionable, they bordered on ridiculous. Men in Bedfordshire would never dream of wearing coats so tight that they could not raise their arms. These striped silk creations looked as though they had squeezed the shirtpoints right up out of the collar. The shirtpoints rode so high they appeared to endanger their wearer's eyeballs. As the men could not turn their necks with ease, they were forced to swivel from the waist to see anything that was not directly in front of them. They looked very much like stiff, wooden dolls made with only one joint. For several minutes Amelia watched an exchange between a man wearing a waist-coat covered with embroidered Chinese cherry blossoms and a man wearing what appeared to be a nosegay the size of a cabbage in his buttonhole.

When she trained her opera glasses upward to the other boxes, she found herself faced with dozens of similar opera glasses all trained upon herself.

"Good heavens! Everyone in the world is looking at me!"

"Sit back, Miss Harrow, and smile," the dowager Lady Westhaven commanded. "Of course they are looking at you. You and Hunter have hardly been out together since the engagement was announced. Everyone just wants to be sure that they get a good look at you."

Amelia resisted the urge to step back into the shadows of the box. "I know how the actors must feel," she laughed. "Perhaps I should launch into a speech decrying Hamlet's abandonment of me." She clutched both hands to her bosom in preparation. Lady Westhaven's eyes widened in horror.

"And my mother could pitch you into the pit for your drowning scene," Hunter said in a conspiratorial underbreath.

"Oh, dear. I think I might impale myself on some of those shirtpoints down there." She peered cautiously down at the milling crowd which continued to move about even when the lights were snuffed out in preparation for the opening scene.

"I think that you are in more danger of Mother's sharp tongue." He laughed softly as his mother stared pointedly down her nose at them. The dowager was too well-bred to shush them in public, but her meaning was clear.

Amelia unfurled her fan in front of her face and peered at Hunter with a roguishly cocked brow. "I will mind my manners, even if everyone else does have the impudence to stare at me."

"How could they not stare, when you are in such good looks tonight?" He skirted the fan and touched her earring so that it swung playfully.

Amelia felt the warmth of his gloved hand long after he had returned it to his lap and turned to watch the play. This was the Hunter she remembered—laughing and kind. She had always been his favorite, and he had always taken care of her. Even when she was a gawky, self-conscious twelve-year-old madly in puppylove with him, he was eternally patient. This elevated him even more in her esteem now, since she realized that the life of a twenty-one-year-old young man does not generally have room for the tender feelings of a neighborhood girl still in the schoolroom.

She looked at his profile in the dimness of the theatre. His hair was cut fashionably short and showed his broad forehead and the dark slash of his brows. His face was sharply formed. It might have been harsh except for the striking darkness of his eyes fringed by straight black lashes. He was watching the stage with an absorbed interest, unconsciously mirroring the expressions of the characters.

She leaned slightly closer to him so that the sleeve of his jacket brushed her bare arm. Even that slight touch made her skin tingle. Hunter patted her hand in an absent but kind manner and continued to watch the play.

The next day was cloudless and warm. It was just the sort of day when everyone in the entire city collectively decided that it is the perfect day to wear their new bonnets and go for a drive in the park. Amelia dawdled over her toilet, knowing that it was considered appropriate for her to be at least a quarter of an hour unready when her fiancé came to call. But it dragged later and later into the afternoon, and there was no word from Hunter.

She had been reduced to lurking at the top of the stairs, when at last she heard a knock at the door. She stood for a moment on one foot, undecided whether to retreat back to her room and play by the rules, or if she could run down and greet him herself. Then she heard a childish voice in the hallway and realized, as her heart tumbled into her stomach, that he was reneging on his promise. Indeed, the note brought by the young boy of the Westhaven household was apologetic and prim.

> *Madam,*
>
> *I regret causing you any inconvenience, but I am unable to take you for a drive as we discussed, as unexpected business has suddenly arisen to detain me. I trust that I will have the honor to drive out with you at another time.*
>
> *I remain respectfully yours, etc.*
>
> *H. W.*

Amelia read the missive again once she was in the privacy of her room. There was no making sense of it. Since when had he called her "madam?" For a moment she conjured up gothic plots involving abduction, blackmail, and men wearing patches over one eye, but there was no room for doubt. The perfect copperplate she knew so well did not contain a secret code. It barely contained civilities.

She should have known. He had hardly sounded interested in the project when she reminded him of the proposed drive last night. She wondered what kind of business he had fabricated to excuse himself. She flounced into the second best drawing room and threw open the lid to the pianoforte. Beethoven? Bach? Something very, very fortissimo. She pounded through several pieces before she started to feel any better.

"You know," said Miriam at last, dropping the book of fashion plates to her lap, "the marvelous thing about a pianoforte is that it plays both forte *and* piano."

"I am sorry, Miriam. I didn't know you were in here." She scowled and went back to playing, but at a lesser volume.

"You're as cross as two sticks."

"Hunter forgot that he was to take me for a drive today and has sent over some perfectly idiotic excuse. I have wasted the entire day waiting for him, when I could have gone out with Harold and Charlotte Macey, since they came by and asked me to accompany them just this afternoon."

"What idiotic excuse did he make?"

"Business suddenly detaining him or some such rot."

"Well, I suppose it is possible," Miriam said doubtfully.

Amelia snorted and began a stinging march. This gave way after some time to a reel that was played at a somewhat more conventional speed and volume, and then to a positively kind minuet.

"Miriam," Amelia began suddenly, stopping the minuet in mid-bar, "what is being married like?"

"Mercy, Amelia! Are you in complete ignorance? Ask Mama, not me!" Her sister took up her book of fashion plates again.

"I didn't mean *that!*" The way she pronounced the word imbued it with every kind of meaning. She accompanied it with a dramatic minor chord. "Besides," she laughed, "you look as though you *should* be asked about that."

"Nonsense, you can't begin to tell yet!" Miriam indignantly pressed her hand to her abdomen.

"Not really," Amelia retracted. "But I imagine that Henry will be able to tell when he is back from Jamaica."

"Of course. He said he could tell before he left. But that, of course, was virtually impossible since I barely knew myself for sure then." She settled back on the sofa with the fashion plates in front of her nose. "Besides," she said after a moment, "you should not speak of such vulgar things." She aimed a remonstrative frown at her sister over the pages.

"I only asked what it was like to be married. You were the one who brought up everything carnal."

Miriam gave a faint shriek of protest. "You are hopelessly crass, Amelia, and it is a wonder that anyone wants to marry you. Mama has let you run hopelessly wild since I was married. The way you and Jack carry on, you would think you were a pair of bear cubs. I look forward to being removed to my own home again once Henry returns."

"Don't be such a stiff-corset. I really do want your advice." She crossed her wrists and played the opening of the minuet with reversed treble and bass.

Her sister sighed and put down the book. "On what about marriage specifically?"

"Do you think that Hunter will be good to me?"

"Good to you?" Miriam's brows rose in confusion. "Of course. If you mean he won't beat you or shout. Of course he won't. You have known him forever."

"Will he take me to balls, and the opera, and outings to the country? I mean, he will spend time with me, won't he?"

"Of course! Of course he will escort you places on occasion. Whatever gave you the idea that he wouldn't? You will be obliged to throw dinner parties together at least once a fortnight." Miriam thought for a moment. "It won't be like now, though."

"No?" Amelia asked with some relief, leaving the pianoforte and sitting beside her sister.

"Well, he is still courting you now, in a manner. When you are married, you must not expect to see so much of him."

"What?" Amelia heard her voice rise to a squeak. "I will see less of him?"

"Don't be a goose. You know that you cannot expect him to dance attendance on you all of the time. Men have their—their men things to do. Horse trading, smoking, beating each other senseless at Jackson's Boxing Salon . . ." She shrugged lightly. "Besides, it is not at all the thing for a man to be seen too much in the company of his wife."

"Why not?"

"Why not?" Miriam echoed in surprise. "It is just not the thing. You would not want him to appear to be completely in your pocket, would you?"

"No . . ." she agreed with reluctance, rising again and returning to the pianoforte.

"Amelia. You are acting childish. I know that you have worshipped the ground that Hunter walks on since you were in leading strings, but you are a grown woman now, and you must get the foolish notions of love out of your head."

"Must I?" Amelia's voice was low.

"Yes. You have a fine and noble man who has chosen you to be his wife, and you should strive to be as obliging and pleasant as possible to him without plaguing the life out of him to meet your romantic notions about love."

Amelia did not reply, but began to play again softly.

"Really," her sister continued, in a tone of unimpeachable authority, "he will get quite tired of it."

"Doesn't Henry love you?" Amelia's playing trailed off in a dismal splatter of notes.

"Henry admires me," Miriam stated firmly, as she sat up straighter, "for my strength of character."

"Oh, dear," said her sister, "that sounds simply terrible."

Four

Four

Amelia looked at herself in the chervil glass and was somewhat disappointed that she recognized herself. The sky blue of the morning dress was draped with silver tissue held in artful rushings with midnight blue ribbons. The modiste had called it an Illusion Gown. She should not have been surprised at it, as she had chosen it carefully with her mother, but she had hoped that when she put it on her wedding day that it would transform her into . . . well, into the gracious, self-possessed married woman she had somehow always wished she would become.

But beneath the carefully dressed dark ringlets at the crown of her head was the same face.

"You look beautiful, Amelia," her mother beamed as she revolved around the dress, smoothing and fluffing its contours. "Now, take your gloves and let's be off. I can see the carriage waiting. Your father has gone ahead to meet us at the church."

Miriam joined them belowstairs, twitching her skirt in annoyance. "I don't know why you could not find someone else to stand as witness for you, Amelia. I am not fit to go out in public in my present . . . condition." She pulled at the seams of her gown as though they were growing tighter as she spoke.

"Nonsense," Lady Harrow said. "You are quite presentable, and it is perfectly acceptable for you to go out for weeks and weeks to come. You are a good deal too particular at times, Miriam."

"Besides, I want you beside me. No one else will do." Amelia linked her arm with her sister's and guided her to the door. She cast one look over her shoulder at the hall mirror and then closed her eyes tightly. That was the old Amelia. She would never be Miss Harrow again.

The heat in the coach was stifling and the lack of conversation made its interior seem even more airless. Amelia kept her eyes fixed out the window.

"I cannot believe my baby girl is getting married. You hardly seem more than a child. But I myself was married at eighteen. And had Miriam at nineteen." She gave a nostalgic sigh. "Are you nervous, my dear?"

"No, Mama, not at all. I have been looking forward to this day for so long. Hunter will be my husband. How funny that sounds! I suppose that I am a little nervous. It is strange that it is finally happening and my dream is coming true."

Her mother smiled, but did not reply immediately. "Your life will probably not be the fairy tale that you imagined," she said at last, "but Lord Westhaven is a good man, and it is a most satisfactory match."

This was probably said to comfort her, but somehow it did not. She clenched her gloved hands in her lap and tried not to think. It would be better to only experience. Thinking only meant being aware that this was the single most irrevocable thing she had ever done in her life.

The carriage arrived at Hanover Square and Amelia was the last to step out onto the pavement. It was a bright and cloudless morning, and the pavement and steps of the church were blindingly reflective. Just as her eyes were becoming accustomed to the light, they

entered the dimness of the church, and she could see
nothing.

It was always annoying to her later that she could
remember virtually nothing of her own wedding. When
she joined Hunter at the altar he had looked so serious
that she was a little frightened. He had looked like she
imagined a man going into battle would look: straight
and tall, with a calm that was broken only by a slight
whiteness about the mouth. But now he sat beside her
at the wedding breakfast at her parent's town house,
and he was her husband. She smiled at him and felt
her heart press against her lungs with a kind of painful,
pinching joy.

"Well, Lady Westhaven, are you ready?"

Amelia felt herself grinning stupidly at him. "That
sounds so nice. Ready for what?"

"Our guests will expect us to leave soon."

"Oh, yes, Hunter, I am ready."

Receiving his new son-in-law's intentions via raised
questioning brows and glances toward the door, Lord
Harrow stood up and addressed the company: "I have
known Hunter Westhaven since he first came squalling
into this world, and I have seen him grow up to be a
fine man. Nothing pleased me more than when he
asked me for my youngest daughter's hand, since it had
become obvious even to me that she had conceived a
partiality for him beyond the admiration the rest of our
family felt.

"I hesitated to approve their betrothal only because
I knew that young Westhaven was off to join our troops
on the Peninsula due to what I thought at the time was
folly for an older son and an excess of patriotism. I did
not want my daughter to hang her hopes on a young

man who might be . . . away for a . . . very long time."
Here Lord Harrow cleared his throat uncomfortably.

"Mentioned in many dispatches and known for leading a company of the Light Dragoons through the thick-
est of fighting Ciudad-Rodrigo, Westhaven is indeed a
hero. And a hero is the only kind of man good enough
for Amelia. I want to be the first to wish them a long
and happy life together."

Her father toasted them and then sat back down beside her. "There now, Petal, don't start crying. Westhaven will beat you for certain if you turn into a
complete watering pot at the least thing." He gave her
a watery smile of his own and squeezed her shoulder.
"You should take your leave now, madam. I saw your
coach arrive fully ten minutes ago."

"Thank you, Papa," she whispered, wishing she could
convey to him the welter of conflicting emotions she
felt. But he was not a man who was comfortable with
an excess of sensibility, so she kissed him on the cheek
and rose along with her husband.

She felt his warm hand clasp hers and realized then
how cold her own was. It occurred to her that this was
the first time she had touched his bare hand with her
own. It seemed a very intimate thing to be doing before
a crowd of people. The pressure of his hand made her
aware of the ring she wore. The delicate gold filigree
band was generations old in Hunter's family. She bowed
and smiled until she thought her cheeks would split
open. At last they were allowed to leave. Miriam was the
last to embrace her as they stepped into the carriage.

"Amelia, I am so happy that you are happy," she stammered. Amelia was surprised to note that she was crying. "Don't bother with what I said before. You go and
be as in love with your husband as you want to. Don't
mind how unfashionable or common it is." She patted

her sister's cheek through the open coach window and at last allowed the coachman to drive on.

Amelia sat back with a sigh. It was over. She could still hear the guests calling their good wishes after them in the street, but at last she was alone with Hunter. It struck her suddenly that they had rarely been alone together.

"It went well, don't you think?" She smoothed her gloves in her lap anxiously.

"Very. Though there was hardly anything that could go wrong. People get married every day. It is not as though one needs special training."

"No, though perhaps one should," she said seriously. "Besides, it is not me who gets married every day."

"No, only today, so I hope you enjoyed it. You are mine from now on, Brat."

"Don't call me by that horrid name," she protested, giving him a dig with her forefinger.

"Oh, but I shall call you by any name I please from now on. I am your lord and master, and I am not going to let you forget it."

She laughed. "You have always been my lord and master, Hunter. And I have never given you any trouble."

"You have never been anything but trouble, Miss Nosey." He pinched that part of her physiognomy.

"Miss Nosey! I hated that nickname even more than Brat!"

"Oh, but you were a Miss Nosey. You always wanted to do whatever I was doing, and echo whatever I was saying, and be in on whatever I was planning. I grew up without a moment's peace because of you, Miss Nosey." He laughed, and Amelia realized that it had been a long time since she had heard it.

"Well, I'm Mrs. Nosey now," Amelia interjected wryly.

She leaned her head against his shoulder and he smoothed her hair. It had been dressed with orange blossoms, and he pulled one out and smelled it. He then put it under her nose for her to smell. She laughed and pressed closer to him, and he put his arm around her shoulders.

"Put it in your buttonhole," she suggested.

He complied. "I will never wear bachelor's buttons again," he announced grandly, pulling out that offensive bloom from the buttonhole. "I must say, Mrs. Nosey, that you looked very beautiful today in the church."

"You are very kind, sir," she replied, more pleased than he knew. She breathed in the smell of him. His arm around her made her feel so safe. He had never embraced her before, except for the most brief and proper occasions, and now, at last he seemed relaxed.

"I had planned that we would spend tonight at our town house here in Town and then go on tomorrow to Crownhaven."

Amelia felt her color rise at the thought of what tonight would entail.

"My mother will stay with Thomas," he interjected, anticipating the objection she was trying to form. "But I did tell her that, as we will most likely stay at Crownhaven for several weeks, she may stay at the town house for that time. Do you mind?"

"No, of course not. I would feel terrible if I thought I were ousting her from her own house."

"It is your house now. She is delighted that I am finally married. She has already had her things moved to the Dower House at Crownhaven."

"You are very thoughtful, Hunter."

They had arrived at the town house, and Hunter helped her to alight once the steps were down. The servants had assembled on the stairs, and Amelia was formally introduced to them. For the first time, she had a maid of her own. Sarah was new and awkward, but

very intent on doing her duties correctly. She also had
a tendency to wonder aloud at things. After some time
of hearing exclamatory comments on the massiveness
of her luggage, the grandeur of her dresses, the thick-
ness of her hair, and the glamor of being mistress of
Crownhaven, Amelia was very much wishing for some
time alone. It seemed as though too much had happened to her in too short of a time. She was Lady Westhaven now. It was peculiar to think about that.

The wedding breakfast had lasted until late in the
afternoon, so they decided to dispense with town hours
and have an early dinner. After so much excitement in
the afternoon, there was very little left for them to do
for the rest of the day. *Except consummate the marriage,*
Amelia added to herself. She felt as though her stomach
were being wrung like a dishrag.

It took nearly an hour for Sarah to manage to get
her ready for dinner. She dashed out of her room and
scampered down the stairs, aware that the dinner bell
had rung ten minutes before. Hunter stepped out of
the drawing room just as she bounded up to the door.

"Ah," he said, smoothing her blown curls, "I thought
perhaps you had fallen asleep."

"No, no, I was just late. I am sorry. It will not happen
again."

"I shall have to beat you this time just to make sure,"
he replied cheerfully, offering her his arm.

The dinner might have been delicious; Amelia didn't
taste a bite. She tried valiantly to keep up a steady
stream of pleasant conversation, but it was difficult.
Hunter always answered readily and agreeably, but he
did not seemed disposed to talk.

She and Hunter had never played at being adults together. Their relationship had always been an informal
thing, consisting of Hunter's avuncular teasing and her
own dog-like devotion. At last they lapsed into silence,

maintaining the conversation only when the servants were in the room.

Amelia was softly playing the pianoforte when he joined her after dinner. It seemed that he remained alone with the port bottle for a long time after she had withdrawn, but he did not appear to have taken too much to drink.

"Please continue," he said, indicating her stilled fingers.

Amelia complied. She finished that piece and began another. Hunter picked up a book. The gilt Louis XIV clock on the mantel seemed to have something wrong with its works. Its ticking was very loud and slow. But no matter how slowly it ticked, it got later, and with each decisive count, Amelia felt more anxious. She felt like crying out to Hunter to just take her to bed and be done with it.

Hunter seemed absorbed in a pamphlet emblazoned with the titillating title *Fallow No More: A Practical Guide to Crop Rotation*. He looked up after a moment, and she realized that her playing had slowed and gradually ground to a discordant stop.

"Shall we retire?" he asked, in the most conversational of tones.

She did not trust her voice, so she merely nodded and stood up. She felt his hand at the back of her waist as they ascended the stairs, but was not really comforted by the warm shivers the pressure evoked.

She found herself wishing that they were on a more even footing. She had known him all of her life, but he was not exactly a friend. She could not confide her terrors to him. She wondered if it were better for brides who did not know their husbands at all when they married. At least they did not have to worry about disappointing the man they loved.

At the door of her chambers, she turned to him with a poise she did not feel. "I will expect you."

His chambers connected to hers through his dressing room. It struck her as very funny that she and Hunter would part at one door and then rejoin each other via another one a few moments later. She was slightly surprised to find Sarah anxiously awaiting her.

"Well, milady?" she asked breathlessly.

It took Amelia a moment to realize that she was 'milady.' She looked at the girl in some confusion.

"Which nightrail will you wear?"

"What? Oh, I don't suppose I care. You pick any one." She began to pull pins haphazardly from her hair and drop them in a china bowl. Sarah seemed positively frenetic. She squeaked in protest when she saw her mistress de-coifing her own hair and rushed to finish it.

Amelia winced under her heavy-handed brushing, but said nothing. She allowed the girl to untie the tapes of her dress, but then dismissed her for the night. It was too hard to concentrate with someone fluttering about her like that.

Taking up the brush, she gave her hair a few last strokes to soothe her injured scalp. She wished briefly that Miriam was with her, but then again, Miriam would probably tell her she was being a goose. She took off her gown and carried it to the clothespress.

The candle on the dressing table fluttered and the door connecting Hunter's dressing room closed softly. Amelia clutched her gown in front of her.

"I—I'm not quite ready, Hunter," she stammered. "Perhaps you could come back later."

"I will help you."

It was so strange to see him in a dressing gown. She recognized his head, but nothing else about him. This was going to be worse than she had anticipated. To her relief, he blew out the candle before he approached her. It was so dark. She could see nothing but the bright orange ember of the candle and a sliver of gray sky at the window where the drapes did not meet. Then she felt him beside her and forced herself not to retreat when he took the gown from her.

He ran his hands lightly down her arms and took her hands in his own, but he did not kiss her. As he led her to the bed, she was grateful that it was dark. She did not want to feel that this was Hunter. Perhaps it was, but she wanted to keep her memory of the grand, heroic Hunter separate from the man that was going to complete this carnal business of bedding.

She lay down, wondering if she was seriously breaching protocol by embarking on this in her chemise rather than the nightgown bought specially for the purpose. The mattress shifted as he lay down beside her, and she did not know if she should have moved to the other side of the bed when she first lay down, so that he would have room. Perhaps to lie where he had put her was rude. Were the covers to be on or off? Was she supposed to make conversation during this? Perhaps she had not been listening when her mother had informed her as to the specifics of the operation.

Hunter moved over to her and embraced her. It was strange to feel his body down the entire length of hers. When had he taken off his dressing gown? She tried to put her arms around him, but found that she was lying on one of them. She held him awkwardly with one arm. His back was warm and smooth. She was unsure if she was supposed to caress him, so she kept her hand where it was. She had somehow thought that instinct would take over at some point in this process. She hoped that it would very soon.

He began to move his hands across her skin, but it

felt ticklish and strange. She wanted to pull away, but she resisted. He kissed her, but when she did not respond, he stopped.

"Kiss me, Millie," he murmured against her mouth.

She tried to sound calm, but her voice came out like a sob. "Please. Just do it."

She felt the muscles in his back twitch but he did not reply. It was too dark to see his expression. She felt him pull her chemise up around her waist and pressed her face into his neck. His breathing sounded very loud above her head.

Somehow he rolled her onto her back and positioned himself between her legs. She wished desperately that he would say something: explain how it was going to feel, direct her on how to proceed, soothe her with assurances that it would be over quickly. She heard a squeaking sound and realized that she was grinding her teeth.

"I will try to make it easy for you," he said gently.

She had promised herself that when it came to it, she would not struggle, but she had thought that the pain would be short and sharp rather than a continuous, searing ache. She tried to escape from under him.

"Still. Be still," he commanded. His voice was thick and did not sound like his own.

She obeyed and lay flat with her hands clenching fistfuls of bed linen. After a few moments, he expelled his breath, shuddered, and stopped thrusting. He was heavy on top of her, but she still did not move. It was very quiet. She could hear the wood in the house contracting after the heat of the day with pops and creaks. She would have liked to have curled up and nursed the pain that continued even after he rolled away from her, but it seemed impolite, so she lay where she was and waited for him to say something. He was silent for so long that she thought he might have fallen asleep.

"I know that I hurt you," he said at last. It was Hunter's voice again. "I'm sorry. It will not be so bad the next time."

The idea of repeating this ordeal made Amelia's stomach ache. "It was not so bad," she replied evenly.

He cleared his throat. "Thank you, my dear. You have made me very happy to have married me today." He kissed her lightly on the mouth.

He sounded as though he were reading from an etiquette book. She felt him get out of the bed. He came around to her side of the bed, and she could see from his silhouette that he was wearing his dressing gown again. She was still lying naked on her back with the sheets wadded on each side of her. He smoothed her hair, the only gesture he had made that did not seem perfunctory, and then she heard him quietly shutting the dressing room door.

That was it. She was officially a woman. She had done her wifely duty. Pulling the coverlet over her head, she allowed herself to curl up at last. It was hard to believe that she had waited all of her life for this. Her dreams of marriage had not included lying alone and in pain on the marital bed. And somehow when she had become betrothed to Hunter, she had assumed that she would not be marrying a stranger.

Five

"How do you do, my dear?" Hunter looked up from the newspaper.

"Very well, thank you. And you?" Amelia looked over the food on the sideboard with disinterest and sat down at the breakfast table with a plate of toast.

"Very well. I hope you slept well."

Her head jerked up in surprise, but he was calmly stirring cream into his tea. Obviously this was meant only as a commonplace remark.

"Very well," she lied perfunctorily. Of course she should never have expected that he would have stayed last night. As Miriam would have said, it was not the done thing. But somehow she had assumed that, as he had known her for so long and been such a patient, understanding mentor in every other way. . . . But that had been a long time ago, and this was an entirely different matter than learning how to drive a pony cart or conjugate Italian verbs.

"I see things are continuing to fair well for Wellington in Spain. God, how I wish I was there!"

Amelia started to ask him why, but he did not look up. Evidently he meant this exclamation to be rhetorical. The paper continued to fascinate Hunter until a footman came in to announce that the coach carrying their baggage and personal servants was nearly ready to leave.

Hunter looked up from the paper and saw Amelia as though for the first time. "I thought I made it clear that we were leaving directly after breakfast. You should have worn a traveling dress. Finish up and then have your maid help you change before she leaves. We can be at Crownhaven before it is very dark if we do not dawdle."

Feeling chastised, she left her breakfast and went upstairs to change her clothing. Sarah had laid out her carriage dress and helped her into it. It was very hard to listen to her rattle, but the girl did not seem to mind that her monologue went unanswered.

At last Hunter handed her into the coach, and they set out. It was very early, and the streets were empty of carriages. Only the drays and vans that supplied the houses of West End with their bread, milk, and meat were plying their trade in the white veil of the morning mist. Servants were removing shutters and sweeping the steps of the great, silent houses. Amelia felt as though she were looking at the innards of a machine before the shiny veneer of Quality awoke and adorned the fashionable end of town with a veritable excess of Good Taste.

It was cool in the carriage, and Amelia sat with a brick under her feet and a coach blanket across her knees. Westhaven spurned the brick and blanket, but wore his driving coat.

"Do you intend to drive the coach today?" Amelia asked, indicating that article.

"Perhaps. It is mostly pretension on my part. I generally do drive myself or ride."

"It is kind of you to travel with me." She leaned affectionately on his shoulder.

Hunter drew back and looked at her with some surprise. "Well, of course. It is the right thing to do." He shifted uncomfortably. "Are you quite comfortable? It will get warmer you know, once the sun has burnt off this mist. In fact, I suspect it will be very warm today indeed."

Amelia acknowledged that he was most likely correct about this, but could offer no other comment.

"Perhaps you would like to go to sleep for a while. We were up very early, and the journey is quite long. I hope that you do not mind that we are to do it in one day. I thought that doing so would be ultimately more comfortable than spending a night somewhere along the way."

"I don't mind."

"I have never actually made this trip in a closed coach." He rubbed imaginary dust from the window with his handkerchief.

Amelia felt as though it were her fault that he was forced to travel at a snail's pace cooped up in a swaying compartment with all the size and comforts of an unlined hat box. "Why don't you drive for a while," she suggested after a long silence interrupted only by Hunter attempting to find a comfortable way to stretch out his legs.

"I think I will," he replied with some relief.

He did so for several hours. Amelia tried to read, but the motion of the carriage made her feel seasick. Needlework was as unappealing as the scenery after awhile, so she resigned herself to an uneasy sleep.

The afternoon was hot indeed, but Hunter manfully rejoined her within the coach. After some attempt at conversation, he leaned his head back and closed his eyes. Amelia let him pretend to be asleep for quite some time.

"Were you nervous about getting married?" she asked as last. Yesterday afternoon when they rode from the wedding breakfast at her house to his, he had seemed so much more relaxed. Was he uncomfortable after the disaster of last night? Perhaps she should reassure him.

He opened his eyes and regarded her for a moment. "Not particularly." He stared absently out the window. "It would be so much more pleasant to ride," he announced with a sigh. "Do you mind if I open the window?"

"Of course not." Amelia clasped her hands in her lap and arranged her feet so that her toes were pointing forward. "I only asked if you were nervous because you are now embarking into married life. It is the great unknown." She was surprised to hear that her laugh sounded a little shaky.

"Such schoolgirl notions . . ." He patted her cheek indulgently. "Are you certain that you are not disappointed that we will not take a honeymoon tour in Europe? Your romantic hopes are not being battered repeatedly with each step the team takes away from Dover?"

Amelia touched her cheek where his hand had been. "No, of course not. Mama says that Europe is dangerous right now. I would not put you in danger again for all the world. I want to spend the rest of the season with you at Crownhaven." She gave another short laugh. "I would like to spend the rest of my life with you at Crownhaven." She took his hand from his knee and pressed it between her own hands. He did not resist, but his eyebrows began to gravitate toward each other.

"I was thinking to take up my seat in Parliament."

"Really? How wonderful. I shall be a political wife. Of course you would not wish to start this session and next session does not start until next spring."

"Perhaps I will start this session," he replied, looking

out the window. "I was thinking of spending a few weeks at Crownhaven and then going back to Town."

"Oh. Well. I would certainly be happy to go back to Town." Somehow his hand had escaped hers and had returned to its former position.

"You would not have to come."

"Of course I would. I would not wish to stay at Crownhaven on my own. Why would you think that?"

"You could have Miriam come and stay with you. And your home is just a few minutes' ride away. Stop making it out as though I am going to lock you up in a tower in the Scottish Highlands or some such thing."

Amelia had never noticed before that his eyebrows seemed to spend much more time creeping toward each other than in their rightful place. "I will go with you whenever you decide to return to Town," she replied firmly.

"As you wish."

They sat in silence for a long time. Amelia felt as though they had quarreled, but it was not as though they had actually disagreed over anything. She schooled her features into calm, pleasant lines. It was so easy to fall back into bad habits with Hunter. All her life she had followed him about and plagued him to pay attention to her. He had always been patient, but now . . . now she wanted their relationship to be one of equals. She wanted him to admire her and want to spend time with her rather than just tolerate the attentions of an infatuated child.

They stopped to change horses and Hunter bespoke a private parlor. Amelia sipped her lemonade and made pleasant conversation regarding the state of the roads, the inn, the parlor, the weather, and the happy likelihood of reaching Crownhaven before dark. Hunter was attentive and agreed wholeheartedly with every remark.

It was painfully obvious that he was not listening to a word that she said.

Hunter stepped into the parlor at Crownhaven a few minutes after the dinner bell rang and found Amelia waiting for him. She stood by the hearth with her head bowed, but she looked up when he entered. He was not sure what to expect after this afternoon's awkwardness, but she smiled easily at him. She was beautiful. He remembered the day when he had realized that. She had only been about fourteen, and he had come back from the Oxford Lent term. He had been almost frightened of the change in her. The roundness of her cheeks, her voice and child's body were gone, and in their place was the beginnings of a young lady with a low, soft voice, a slim and well-formed figure and eyes such a surprising green.

Of course she had green eyes. How could he have forgotten? He felt vaguely as though he had forgotten many things. There was something strange about being again in this house, where he had so many memories—happy ones, which had not surfaced in his consciousness since Ciudad-Rodrigo. Since long before that. It was strange that he had not missed home while he was in Spain. He had not missed Amelia, either. It was as though he had closed off that part of his past and was only now awakening to it. He felt an unexpected surge of longing for home and family, even though he was already home.

He noticed that Amelia was regarding him with an expression of perplexity. "Shall we go in to dinner?" He chided himself for falling into a reverie in the middle of the doorway and resolved to be particularly pleasant at dinner to make up for his lack of conversation in the coach. And for last night. He winced inwardly.

That had been a tactical disaster. He had gone into it with every intention of making the experience as love-filled and pleasant as possible for her, but she had lain there passionlessly unresponsive. The only time she had moved was when she was struggling to get away from him—as though he were raping her! It had not been a pleasant experience for either of them. He wondered that someone who seemed to think he was some kind of mythical hero could be so entirely, humiliatingly unaffected by his attempts at lovemaking.

Amelia smiled and took his arm, but she did not say anything.

"Do you find your chambers to be to your satisfaction?"

"Yes, they are lovely."

"Of course you will want to decorate them according to your own taste. In fact, you may do whatever you want with the house. It is your home now."

They began with the fish. "Thank you," she said.

"And Sarah, will she suit you?"

"Absolutely." Amelia smiled warmly.

There was a long silence, made louder by the sound of cutlery on china.

"My mother and Thomas are likely to stay in London for the remainder of the season."

"How pleasant for them."

"In the autumn, my mother will, of course, be nearby at the Dower House, and I daresay that she will like to visit here. I hope that you have no objections."

"None at all," she replied affably.

Hunter gave up trying to draw her into conversation and applied himself to carving the beef.

He joined her in the drawing room after dinner. He knew he had lingered too long over his port, but he felt a kind of unnamable dread of spending the evening in the drawing room making polite conversation. Whose genius idea was it that man and wife should spend time alone together after their marriage? It should be just the opposite. They should be gradually eased into each other's company and should spend the first few weeks never having to address each other in private.

With his hand upon the door to the drawing room, he wished briefly that he had married a stranger. It was hell to have to look into Amelia's worshipful eyes and know that eventually the love there would turn to disappointment. He entered the room with a stiff smile. There were times when he hated her for loving him.

Amelia had never thought that she would be grateful for being forced into pianoforte lessons, but to camouflage the silence this evening, she played for several hours. Merciful heavens, if this continued, she would be forced to take up the harp. At last, she tentatively announced her intention to retire.

Hunter looked up from *A Guide to the Cultivation of Mangel Wurzel and Other Beet Crops,* in which he had been engrossed at the same page for almost an hour. He stood and approached her. Amelia braced herself for the events to come.

"Good night," he said, pressing a passionless kiss on her brow. "I think that I will stay up and read. I will see you in the morning."

Amelia closed the door behind her and mounted the stairs to her room. Did that mean that he would not come to her tonight? She felt relieved and rejected at once.

Once Sarah had unfastened the tapes of her gown, Amelia dismissed her and sat alone at her dressing table. She stared blankly into the glass and methodically brushed her dark hair into submissive waves. Poor Hunter. He seemed so unhappy, so unable to relax. She tried to remember what he had been like in the years before the war, but it was difficult. One did not generally inquire into the thoughts and feelings of a demigod.

She began to plait her hair into a prosaic braid. She could make him happy. She would do anything. It would just mean trying harder and figuring out what it was that made him . . . irritable. Perhaps she should speak to the cook. Papa's crochets were generally caused by bilious upsets brought on by too many sauces. She stuffed the braid into her nightcap and padded over to the big, empty bed.

Six

The next weeks fell into a pattern that, if it was not exactly comfortable, was a pattern. Each morning, Amelia awoke and assessed the weather. If it was fine, she might walk in the shrubberies, or ride on the estate or into the town of Little Hissings. If it rained, she would read, or sew, or torture the housekeeper by begging to be allowed to do something. Today, when she drew back the heavy, green velvet curtains, a great splat of rainwater blew at the window like a sneeze. She sighed as she watched the shrubberies heave with the gusts of wind and the lawn flatten in waves like the sea. Mrs. Egan, the housekeeper, must have looked out the window this morning with the same sense of dread.

She rang the bell for her chocolate and shrugged into a dressing gown. For the first few days she had gone down to breakfast, but Hunter was always up and gone. Eating alone in the breakfast room was far too depressing an ordeal to continue. When her chocolate arrived, she sipped it meditatively and considered her options. Hunter went out in every weather and was not likely to come home, even for luncheon. He preferred to carry a satchel of food with him for his midday meal, as if he were on campaign as he toured the estate.

He would be home just before it turned dark, but Amelia had ceased to look forward to his arrival. He

ate silently and then, after dinner, roamed about the
room like a caged animal while she sat in the silent
parlor. Generally he could stand this for about three
quarters of an hour before he announced that he had
letters to write or papers to oversee and retired to his
study.

"Mrs. Egan says that you might like to spend some
time today looking about the attic," Sarah announced
as she helped her mistress into a plain day gown. "She
says that today she is counting linen, and no, she
doesn't need help, and no, she can't be disturbed."

Amelia opened her mouth to protest.

"Cook says that you can't make scones today on account of the fact that they are making jam belowstairs.
And no, she doesn't need help, and no, she can't be
disturbed." There was an unservile gleam in Sarah's
eye.

Amelia gave a rueful laugh. "So I am banished to the
attic."

"Mrs. Egan says that there are quite a lot of things
stored there, and you should decide what you would
like to do with them." Sarah smiled encouragingly. "It
is a good thing that you are wearing that old gown. I
daresay that there is a frightful lot of cataloging to do
up there."

"No doubt there is," Amelia replied unenthusiasti-
cally.

Sarah nodded and turned to go. She paused with her
hand on the doorknob. "I was thinking, ma'am," she
began hesitantly. Seeing Amelia's raised brows she continued. "I was thinking that perhaps you could hire
yourself a genteel companion. I hear that that is what
is generally done. That way you would have yourself
someone to talk to."

"And I wouldn't keep bothering the staff," Amelia
finished. She laughingly shooed the girl out, but her

animated expression fell the moment she was alone in the room. Yes, she could hire a companion. She could even have Miriam come over from Harrow End to keep her company. But it seemed a shabby thing to have to dredge up a companion on one's honeymoon. Perhaps it would have been better if she had insisted on some kind of trip, not to Europe, of course, but perhaps to the Lake District or Scotland. Then she would have been assured a measure of Hunter's attention for at least a few weeks.

She took a sheaf of foolscap and the rest of her writing implements and made her way to the attic stairs. Not a very exciting honeymoon, to say the least. But she had thought that it would be more romantic to stay secluded at Crownhaven with their privacy assured by the fact that it was the middle of the London season. She had not bargained on Hunter's restlessness. He had thrown himself into estate management as though the place were in shambles instead of running like a power loom under Thomas's careful stewardship.

She was unprepared for the state of the attics. They were nothing like the dusty, cobwebbed troves of mystery that gothic novels boasted. They were bright and clean and disappointingly well-organized. She could have discharged Mrs. Egan on the spot. She realized with further disappointment that the dowager Lady Westhaven would surely have gone through all of her belongings stored here before she removed to the Dower House. Any tattered diaries containing dastardly plottings, mysterious portraits of lost heirs, or diamond necklaces hidden in secret compartments of ancient dressing cases would have been found, dusted, and neatly put away. Curse those tidy, thorough Westhavens!

After looking half-heartedly into several of the trunks and finding nothing more mysterious than old books of accounts and the plans for a new stable (which was

now at least half a century old), she found a trunk filled
with clothes. There was a court dress so heavy that she
could not remove it from the trunk. It was embroidered
with a peacock pattern of pearls and gems. Although
court style had not changed so very much, she guessed
from the enormity of the panniers and the long fall of
lace from the sleeves that it must have been made at
the time when Hunter's mother made her bows. It was
hard to imagine that stately, exacting woman nervously
preparing for the occasion.

She pushed the dress to one side and found a small
pile of christening gowns. Several were falling to pieces
and brownish yellow from age, but one at least was in
good condition. Amelia fingered the delicate lace hem-
ming the long skirt. Perhaps her own children would
wear this. She smiled when she felt a blush rise to her
cheeks even in the solitude of the attic. It was possible
that she would become pregnant soon. Hunter visited
her at night several times a week. His lovemaking did
not hurt her anymore. In some ways she found herself
looking forward to it. It was the only intimacy they
had—those strange, breathless encounters in which she
lay still and obedient beneath him.

But she would not think of Hunter now. It was too
sad. Too frustrating. She dug through the rest of the
trunk but the remaining clothes were uninteresting.
Doubtless they were stored for sentimental reasons of
some sort, but it was hard to imagine why someone
would want to keep a pair of gardening gloves or a worn
out pair of knee breeches in a shade of puce that could
not have flattered any human on the earth.

The trunk behind the one with the clothes was very
much more interesting. It had originally been painted
in yellow lettering with "Very Private Property of John
Hunter Kirby Westhaven" but most of the paint had
flaked off long ago. Inside was a tumbled collection of

storybooks, toys, copybooks and a rather ghastly insect collection contained in small, neatly labeled jars. Amelia felt a vague rush of guilt. Here was an intimate look at a side of Hunter she did not know. His own childhood had nearly past by the time she remembered him, and she had never thought of him as ever having been a little boy. Because of the nine years between them, her version of Hunter was always old and clever and divinely above any of her own childish games.

She picked up a wooden cup set on a handle. A string around the handle was attached to a ball. The toy's bright colors were worn away entirely at the handle. She made several unsuccessful attempts to catch the ball in the cup, then set it aside. There was a set of jackstraws, a deck of cards with ships painted on their pasteboard backs, and a truly marvelous regiment of tin soldiers in their own wooden box. Amelia studied each object intently, hoping somehow to divine from them a glimpse of Hunter's past.

Carefully setting aside a wooden saber with a wistful smile, she tried to count how many time she had actually seen him when he was home between terms at Oxford. Her memory of him was vivid, but it was mostly in his role as knight errant of her girlish daydreams. She was worshipfully enamorate of him right up to when he left for Spain. Her sad smile had become a tight grimace. Oh, she was pathetic indeed; she had allowed her vague memories of Hunter to grow into a monster of virtues and romantic ideals.

She shook off those thoughts and continued delving into the trunk. Underneath a bundle of cricket bats, tennis rackets, and a croquet mallet painted with the name "The Avenger," was a set of books. Most of these were spellers, history, Italian, and Greek textbooks of the driest sort. One was a blue bound copybook containing Hunter's round childish handwriting. Besides the obligatory grammar and arithmetic, there was a funny moral story about a boy who stole a pear and thereby condemned himself to suffer for the rest of his life incessant, violent, pear-related accidents. There was a paragraph entitled "The South Seas Pirate," which ended abruptly when the writer evidently got bored, and there were drawings.

Amelia exhaled a slow breath of wonder. They were extremely well executed. One was of his dog, whom he had slyly named "Sir," running jubilantly across the lawn, his tongue lolling. She remembered Sir well, and the drawing somehow managed to capture his doggy personality. There were other drawings of views and houses around Crownhaven and several recognizable portraits of tenants. She closed the book and held it to her, wishing that she could use it as a textbook to decipher the man she had married.

"Hunter, you are back." Amelia smiled and held out both hands to her husband.

"How was your day?" he asked, bowing over them perfunctorily.

"I had a fine time. But it is you I am concerned about. You must have been soaked through the whole day." She rang the bell for tea and encouraged him to sit on the sofa.

"I was." He dropped to the seat she indicated and stretched his legs before him. "And to add insult to injury, the entire day was wasted."

"Why?" She seated herself beside him and took his hand in her own.

He did not remove it. "I had planned to supervise the reroofing of several of my tenants' cottages, but of course the rain prevented that. So I rode out to see how the drainage system was fairing in Pye's field and the one adjoining it."

Amelia wished that he had referred to them as "our tenants," but she did not stop him. She gravely nodded and fixed his tea the way he liked it.

"Well, the damned drains weren't working at all. The place is an absolute lake. It looks even worse than before because the drains are blocked further up and so the entire region is swamped. The summer wheat that Thomas put in is going to rot. The tenants are going to be in bad shape this winter, I'm afraid."

"Well, as long as we know that now, we can plan to buy additional stores."

"Yes, yes, of course." He sat still for a moment, his straight black brows meeting. "Damn this rain. It has rained nearly every day. Eddie King broke his leg when his mule slipped in the mud and fell on him. I don't know how they will manage, since he will doubtless be laid up when it comes time to bring their crops in and they only have William to help them. Whatever crops survive this monsoon," he added bitterly.

"Poor Mr. King. I will ride over tomorrow with a basket from Cook."

Hunter looked at her in surprise. "That's very decent of you."

"Well, I think that it is the least I should do."

"You are right. Mama, of course, would have sent something, but I don't think she would have taken it over there herself. She was never one to be particularly . . . friendly with the tenants." He smiled at her and Amelia felt herself go warm at his praise. Hunter sipped his tea and seemed to become more relaxed. "Well enough of me ranting. Tell me what you did today, Milzie."

"Oh, I had the most marvelous time. I was up in the attic trying to undo some of the rampant organization your mother left, and I came across some things of yours."

"Mine?" he smiled faintly.

"Oh, yes, let me get them. I would like for you to explain them to me. You must have cared very much for these toys, since I know you had a great deal more, and yet these were the ones that you packed up in your trunk." She retrieved the articles from a deal table behind the sofa.

"Tell me about these." She handed him the pack of cards.

Hunter laughed as he examined them and Amelia felt a glow of personal triumph. "These were given to me by my Uncle Robert. He was in the navy, and of course these cards inspired in me an instant desire to sail the high seas. For quite some months I was completely unintelligible for all the sea lingo I used. When I told my mother she should 'batten down the mizzen' when the wind made her skirts fly nearly inside out, I thought she would box my ears." He laughed again. "I learned all the card games I know with these cards." He indicated a small crease at the corner of an ace. "I also learned how to cheat."

"You would never cheat!"

"No, but I do know how." He fanned the cards, offered her one, took it back, reshuffled, and promptly produced the same card from her ear.

"I think you missed your calling," she said wryly.

"My cupball!" he exclaimed delightedly, moving closer to Amelia and turning over the various things she held in her lap. She felt a flush of warmth at the contact of his body. "Here is where I missed my calling. I was the cupball champion of Little Hissings." He demonstrated his skill for a few moments. "I'm a little rusty," he explained sheepishly.

He dove back into her collection and lifted up the

box of tin soldiers. The lid was emblazoned with a fierce battle scene involving a highly unlikely jumble of foot soldiers, cavalry, lancers, artillery, and standard bearers.

Hunter considered it for a moment, then snorted with disdain. He peeked inside briefly and then put the box aside. "What a little idiot I was. I loved war. I was obsessed with it. I spent hours staging battles and planning how I was going to cover myself with glory the moment I was allowed to buy a set of colors." The bitterness in his voice alarmed her.

"Tell me about Spain," she asked quietly.

He looked at her for a moment, his dark eyes unreadable. "Spain is a beautiful country. A beautiful country that has been destroyed by the greed of the French and the arrogance of the English. I saw churches that were hundreds of years old destroyed by fires and looting. Most Spaniards could care less who ruled their country, as long as they are allowed to farm their little piece of land. I saw them starve because the army confiscated their food stores. . . ." He seemed to come back to himself. "Don't ask me about Spain again," he said gruffly, rising to his feet and moving to the fireplace.

Knowing that she had unsettled him, she watched him begin the aimless pacing that was so familiar to her.

"I'm sorry, Hunter," she said in a low voice, trying not to sound pleading. "I only wanted to try to fill in the gaps. We grew up together and we have been friends for so long, I feel like I missed those years of your life. Years that were important."

"Important, hah. They were the greatest misuse of my youth conceivable."

"I want to hear about them."

He stood silently at the mantel for so long, she thought he had not heard her. "What do you want to know?" he asked at last.

"Tell me about the day you were wounded."

He unconsciously touched his shoulder. "Twenty-five out of the sixty in our company were killed that day."

"How awful," she said softly.

"It wasn't awful. It was a crime. It didn't have to happen, and I was responsible."

"What do you mean?" she asked, aghast.

"I should have led them better. I should have led them better or died myself doing it." He stared into the empty fireplace.

"Nonsense," Amelia replied bracingly. "People have always died in wars. It is their nature. Those men went into it knowing the risks."

"Yes," he said slowly, "but their families. Most of the families could not even afford to bring their boys back. They don't even know what happened, only that they are dead."

"What do you mean?"

"Well, the commander sends a nice letter saying all the right things. Your son died doing his duty for England and all that, and that is all."

"But I am sure that you said more than that for your men," she said loyally.

"I would have. But I was barely conscious in the field hospital for weeks afterward. Captain Heller wrote the letter. Or rather his secretary did." She saw his jaw tighten. "I would rather not talk about it."

"But you could write the letters now if you wanted. You could remember what happened to those men."

"I don't want to discuss it anymore. It is not a fit subject." He resumed his circuit of the room.

"But I want to know more."

His face grew hard. "Why are you always pushing me to talk about it? It's in the past. Let it stay there."

"Because it still affects us!" she cried. "I don't know you anymore."

"You never knew me."

He must have seen the hurt expression that crossed her face, for he interrupted her words before they left her lips. "I can't talk about it. I know you want to know, but you can never understand. Please know that this is just something I can't explain."

Amelia regarded him warily. He met her gaze for a moment and then stared sullenly out the window. She wanted so much to argue that she didn't want to change him or cure him—she only wanted to hear about it. She wanted to know what inspired his restlessness and bitterness. She wanted to feel that she shared his terrible burden.

She realized that she had used the treasures of his childhood to try to force a confidence from him. She dumped them unceremoniously onto the couch and stood to go. Their eyes met with mutual expressions of anger, pride, and frustration, but he did not call her back when she left the room.

Seven

"Are you sure you don't want to take a groom with you, milady?"

"No, Allan, thank you. If you don't mind, I would rather be on my own today. I know that my usual groom's daughter is visiting with her baby, so I gave him the day off."

"I could send someone else with you," the head groom coaxed, reluctantly leading the mare to the mounting block.

But Amelia gave him a cheerful refusal and took the saddlebag full of provisions for the cottager's family. She rode off, deaf to entreaties that she take the gig instead. It was silly, but she felt the need to be alone. Alone by herself, not alone in the big house surrounded by quietly sympathetic servants.

She set off toward the Kings' house at a brisk trot in order to kick the fidgets out of the mare. Hunter had been gone when she awoke, as usual. She had actually heard him pass the door to her room as the sky was just growing rosy. She had gone as far as to pull on her dressing gown and start downstairs after him, but she could not bring herself to call after him.

After she had left him last night, she had gone up to her room regretting everything she had said. She had left the door to their adjoining dressing rooms slightly ajar, hoping to indicate her openness to reconciliation, but had gone to sleep without much hope. He had come to her late in the night and made love to her as he always did. She was surprised when she felt him slide into the bed beside her, but his presence in her bed did not ever seem to correlate with his mood when they said good night. He visited her room regularly, slipping in after they had parted outside her bedroom door, but he never lit the candles or mentioned it during the daytime. It seemed strange that he would want to sleep with her when she knew he was angry with her. She had been struck with the sudden paranoia that this man was not her husband.

As she crossed the fields with the wind catching her breath and whisking it back down her throat, she felt foolish for the fears she had entertained the night before. Of course it had been Hunter. She knew that form and voice well enough. It was just that his conjugal visits seemed so detached, so unrelated to the strained, distant life they led during the day at Crownhaven. She liked to think that last night his gentleness had been deliberate and that he had spent a little longer with her before he went back to his own room once he was finished. Perhaps it was his silent way of asking her to be patient with him. To wait a little longer for him to open up to her.

She arrived at the Kings' cottage and pushed those thoughts from her mind. A young man mending a fence near the house hailed her with a broad grin.

"Hello, is this the Kings' house?" she asked.

"It is, it is. And I am a King. Ha ha, I am a King." He bowed and nodded and laughed as though this was very, very funny.

"And I am Lady Westhaven. Is Mrs. King at home?"

"Are you now? Lady Westhaven?" He examined her closely and then began bowing and nodding even more vigorously, muttering, "Lady Westhaven, Lady Westhaven" under his breath as though he were trying to commit it to memory.

When he showed no disposition to answer her question, Amelia dismounted by herself and unhooked the saddlebag. "I hear that Mr. King has broken his leg."

"My pa. Yes, he has, yes, he has," he laughed delightedly and followed her toward the house, still ducking. "Broke his leg, he did. Ma is looking after him. We call her the Queen on account of the fact that she is Mrs. King. You have a very nice horse. May I pat her? I love horses very much. I expect you have a lot of grooms up at Crownhaven, but if you were ever, ever in the need of an under groom, you might think of William King, that is me, William King if you ever needed a groom." He spoke very fast and breathlessly.

"How is Mr. King?" she asked, to stop him.

"He is fine. Couldn't be better. Except, you see, he broke his leg. Terrible thing, broken leg. Good thing he isn't a horse. We might have to shoot him, ha ha, shoot him. Lucky thing he is not a horse. I love horses." They paused at the door of the cottage, and, as soon as he was stationary, the young man began to bow again. "Lady Westhaven, Lady Westhaven, Ma, this is Lady Westhaven."

"Lord, ma'am you didn't have to come see us yourself!" Mrs. King exclaimed, savagely shoving her gray hair beneath her cap.

"I came to ask about Mr. King's health. I have brought over a joint, some wine, broth, and some very nice jellies."

Mrs. King looked slightly puzzled. "Why?"

"I—I thought Mr. King might like them . . . while he is convalescing."

"You brought them for *us?*" Mrs. King looked stunned. She regained her composure and invited

Amelia inside where Mr. King lay on the bed with his splinted leg.

"How good of you to come to us, Lady Westhaven," he said, when introduced to her. "Your husband has been to see me several times since the accident. He is a great man, Lord Westhaven. Now, young Lord Thomas was a good manager, but Lord Westhaven is determined to put everything even righter. He practically insisted that we have a new roof and a shed for the pig no matter how I told him we could do without."

Amelia talked for quite a while with Mr. King about their roof, their crops, and their harvest now that he was indisposed. She was surprised how much knowledge of the estate she had picked up just by listening to Hunter. At length she rose to go, amid a renewed chorus of her virtue. She promised to visit them again next week and send over a man to help with the gathering in, when the time came. It seemed as though Mrs. King had her hands full with only the one child to help with the house and the crops. And William did not seem to be as level-headed as his father. In fact, he was hardly ever level at all, since he at once resumed bowing and smiling whenever he caught her eye.

"Thank you, Lady Westhaven. I'm sure Eddie will be right as a trivet soon enough." Mrs. King walked her outside. "But you'd best be getting on now. It looks like the storm is about to break. I'll have William hand you up." William appeared from the smoky interior of the cottage and commenced bowing and nodding in the most convivial manner. Amelia wondered briefly how he would ever contrive to help her onto her mount without making her wildly seasick, since he continued bobbing as he approached.

He managed to seat her with a minimum of scrambling, and she set off, giving a private word of assurance to William that she would speak to her husband about the possibility of hiring another groom. Mrs. King had been right; the weather looked as though it would turn nasty soon. She urged the mare to a quick trot, even as fat raindrops began to splash the saddle and dot her cloak.

An explosion of thunder split the sky directly overhead, and Amelia strained to keep the mare from bolting. The rain was coming down in earnest and a sharp wind had sprung up. Her flapping cloak was spooking the animal more, and it took all of her skill to calm it. The rider was upon her before she even saw him.

"There, there, I've got her." Hunter took the horse's bridle and spoke in a low soothing voice to the mare.

"It's all right, Hunter. I don't need your help," Amelia snapped. Another roar of thunder made the horse throw up her head. Hunter ignored his wife's protests and began to lead the animal by the bridle.

"What are you doing here?" she shouted above the wind, but "mangel wurzel" were the only words she could distinguish in his reply. Sitting up straighter in the saddle, she submitted to the humiliation of having him lead her.

He took them at a quick jog across a field and then stopped. Amelia fought the dripping hair out of her eyes to see that they had arrived at a cottage. Sighing in relief, she slid from the saddle. She sloshed up the muddy, overgrown walk and pounded at the door. The wind was blowing the rain into painfully sharp, wet needles. No one answered her summons, but she was dimly aware that Hunter had led the horses away. The house must be abandoned. She attempted to peer into one of the shuttered windows but only succeeded in stepping into an ankle-deep mire of mud and receiving a sluice of rainwater from the roof pelting onto her ruined riding hat. She returned to the door and pounded again.

"Don't you have the sense to get out of the rain?" Hunter popped out of the door and asked mockingly.

"I didn't think I should just go barging in," she retorted. "How did you get in? What did you do with the horses?"

"I came through the back door. There is a shed at the back." He answered each question in order with a grin. He began to search around the cottage. "I suppose it would be too much to hope that before Mrs. Griggs went to live with her son, she left behind a tidy supply of firewood and several changes of clothes."

"This place has been shut up for quite a long time," Amelia remarked, removing her bedraggled hat. A leak in the roof instantly opened up and began to drip on her bare head.

The room was empty of everything except a few mouse droppings, and it smelled damp and unpleasant. Hunter had disappeared up the stairs, so she took off her cloak and spread it in front of the hearth. It seemed like the logical thing to do, regardless of the fact that no fire had graced that orifice for years.

"Well," said Hunter cheerfully, "I have found quite a treasure. Two stools, one to sit upon and one to burn and"—he paused for dramatic effect—"a horse blanket!"

"Lucky horse," Amelia said dryly between teeth clenched to keep from chattering.

"Gudgeon," he returned. "Your cloak, milady." He draped the offensive object around her shoulders."

"Mmm," she sniffed. "Parfum du cheval, my favorite." She shuffled after Hunter who was fishing in the pockets of his greatcoat for a tinderbox.

"I have taken the liberty of deciding to burn the stool with two legs, while retaining the one with three." While he exuberantly broke the ill-fated stool to kindling, Amelia regarded the survivor with misgivings. Rather than being a three-legged stool, it was a four-legged stool missing one leg. This amputation resulted in the seat tilting at an angle impossible to sit on.

"Is there no way we could use a leg of that one for this?" she asked, attempting to right the stool.

Hunter held up a leg in reply. It was obviously far too long.

"Burn them both then; this one is of no use."

"We'll see." He gave her a smile that seemed far too cheerful for the situation.

"I declare, Hunter, I almost think you're enjoying this," she said ruefully as she pulled off her gloves and stretched out her hands to the warmthless flicker in the hearth.

He looked up from where he crouched. "I am," he said simply. He righted the remaining stool and perched on a corner of it so that it remained upright. "Come and share the blanket with me, you selfish wench." He drew her onto his lap, and Amelia arranged the repulsive blanket around them both.

"Ah, Milz," he said after a long moment, "I was not cut out to be a gentleman. This inactivity has driven me mad. I make a much better soldier than husband, I'm afraid."

Amelia had no answer to this, as she agreed with him to some extent. It was so luxurious, though, to sit in his arms and feel his breath on her neck. The wind rattled the shutters and the roof continued to drip, but the fire was burning warmer now. She pressed herself closer to his chest.

"I wish this were our house," she said softly.

"What? Why? Does the duchess wish to play at being a shepherdess?"

"I'm not a duchess, if you recall," she replied tartly. "Viscountess."

"No, no sheep, if you please. I only sometimes wish

that you weren't so restless. That you had difficult and challenging things to keep you occupied."

"Occupied," he echoed.

"Thomas has run the estate so well that you have nothing to do except wonder if you should devote the north field or the northwest to your precious mangel wurzels."

He smiled. "So you wish we lived instead in a tumbled-down, mouse-infested, leaking hovel?" He smoothed her hair from her face. "You are a strange girl."

"I do," she replied, "just you and I."

"Just you and I," he repeated. But his words were a caress. He kissed her gently on the mouth. It occurred to her that he rarely did so, even when he visited her room late at night. His second kiss was more insistent. When he at last pulled away, she was entirely speechless. He must have seen her stunned expression; his slow smile was self-mocking. "That is how it should be done, my sweet." He brought his finger to her lips and traced their shape with a languid deliberateness.

She gave a little gasp and tried to swallow. She had had no idea that a mere kiss could reduce her to a state of desire that made her frighteningly wild with need. His eyes were so dark she could see her own reflection.

"That was the first time you have kissed me back." He gave a sensual laugh low in his throat. "You have seduced me, Lady Westhaven."

Unaware that she had initiated it, she pulled him to kiss her again. The room seemed to grow very hot, and she could hear her blood throbbing in her ears above the roar of the rain. His hand was at her back pulling her closer, and he parted her lips with his tongue. She stiffened in surprise. This invasion felt far more intimate than even the marital act itself. She tentatively

responded in kind and heard a purr-like moan of pleasure from his throat.

With the hand that was not supporting her, he began
to deftly remove the pins from her hair. It uncoiled in
a thick, dark roll. She found she had entirely destroyed
his neckcloth and pulled three buttons off his waistcoat.
The horse blanket fell away from them unheeded as
she arched her body to his, wordlessly begging him to
continue. He bared her throat of the lace fall there and
began a long exploration of her neck and collarbone.
When he reached her breast, she gave a shuddering
gasp and clenched her hands in his hair to pull his
mouth into even more intimate contact with her body.
His impassioned response to this caused an unfortunate
miscalculation in his balance, and the insulted stool
tipped them both into a tangled heap on the floor.

Amelia gave a short laugh that was more like a pant.
"We should have burned the thing after all." She was
lying on top of him with her hair hanging like a tent
around their faces. He gave an unintelligible exclamation and began to wrest off her habit. She had never
seen him naked in the light before, and she watched
him covertly as he removed her stockings. His propor-
tions were balanced perfection and his skin—her
thoughts were arrested by the sight of the scar tissue
on his shoulder. She knew that he had been wounded,
but he never spoke of it. She wondered if it still hurt
him. Her thoughts did not have long to dwell on this
as he stretched out beside her on the horse blanket and
pulled her to him.

"I won't have you lie there like some martyred saint,"
he said with gentle menace. "This time I'm going to
see that you enjoy yourself."

He did not enter her immediately, but began to touch
her in a way that brought her with excruciating slowness
to a peak of agonized pleasure. This was nothing like

their previous lovemaking. Only when she was reduced to a state of gasping incoherencies did he slowly ease into her body. With hedonistic greed, she ran her hands down the smoothness of his back and pressed him deeper within her. His drew a quick breath and his eyes sank slowly closed.

With his head bent to hers, he began to move within her, murmuring disjointed syllables of desire. His motion was calculated to bring her even more pleasure and at last she gave a cry of triumph and surprise and clung to him in a shuddering climax. She was dimly aware that he, after another thrust, gave a low moan and lay still and panting on top of her.

Eight

Amelia replayed the scene in her mind for days. She ran through everything that they had said, every movement he had made in the hopes of making it seem somehow more real. Unfortunately, the more she thought about it, though her skin grew flushed and her eyes unfocused, the more she felt as though she were making it all up. She tried not to think about what had happened afterward. They had dressed in awkward silence and spent a stilted hour waiting for the rain to stop. She could not understand how, after such a passionate exchange, he could suddenly emotionally withdraw so fully. Hunter now treated her with a courtesy that bordered on stiffness and handed her cups of tea and fetched her shawl as though he wanted to make up for his passion with a smothering blanket of solicitude.

She had hoped at the time that this punctiliously tepid attention would pass, but when they returned to their regular schedule of not seeing each other, she realized that even that attention had been better than nothing. Some nights he visited her in her room, but it was as though the afternoon in the cottage had never happened.

It was nearly a week later, and she had rarely seen him. He had continued in his habits of rising early and staying out all day. Several times she had seen him on the estate as she went out riding or visiting tenants in the gig, but he would only wave at her from a distance and then ride off looking very busy. Their evenings at home consisted of dinners in which Hunter tried to converse pleasantly on neutral subjects, offered her plates of food, and followed her directly to the drawing room when she rose to leave him to his port. He asked her to read aloud to him and then stared unhearing into space. She knew he was trying, but it was so hurtful to think that one's husband must try to remember to be kind to you after only five weeks of marriage.

She rose early, shortly after she heard him creak carefully down the stairs. When she arrived at the stables, most of the grooms were off having their breakfast in the kitchen. Only William King sat in the tack room, industriously rubbing oil into a harness.

"Lady Westhaven, you are here! You are here at last! I have hoped to see you so I could thank you," he exclaimed, leaping to his feet and bobbing.

"For what? For hiring you on as groom?" She passed a hand across her forehead, smoothing away the creases. "It was no trouble. I hope you are happy. Could you saddle the mare for me?"

"Oh, I am very happy. Very happy indeed. I love horses. Yes, I am very happy."

"Good," she smiled, trying not to be impatient. "Could you saddle my mare?"

"Right away, milady," he beamed, bobbing away. "You are up very early. Very early indeed. Milord is just now off, and he is known to be one to rise early. Early as a farmer they say. Yes, early as a farmer."

"I thought I would try to rise earlier myself. I hear that it is beneficial to one's health," she lied.

"So it is; so it is." He saddled the mare with a careful slowness that rankled Amelia. She refrained from beating a tattoo on her boot with her whip.

"Where did Lord Westhaven go?" she asked, with a casual air.

"Weeeeelll." William examined the girth with academic interest. "I think he said he might go look at the stream. With all the rain we have been having lately, he is anxious that the bridge may be washed away."

"That is what I thought." She mounted swiftly and waved her whip cheerfully at William. "There is no need for you to saddle a mount to accompany me. I am off to see the Wheelers." She gave the mare her head, and the animal set off at a quick trot. Once she was over the hill, she changed direction and headed toward the stream. She tried to concentrate on the freshness of the morning rather than her anxiety. It was impossible. How could Hunter possibly be so absorbed by the estate? Did he have a "bit o' muslin" he was slipping off to visit?

The idea made her feel ill, and she pressed her knee against the mare to urge her forward. At last the stream came into sight; its sparkling shine seemed out of place in the overcast morning. Amelia's lungs collapsed in a sigh of relief when she saw Hunter's horse lounging in a bored attitude by the wooden bridge. She could vaguely make out Hunter as he scrambled down the bank.

She was overwhelmed with shame. How could she have doubted him? She stopped the mare behind a stand of willows and watched while her husband made a thorough examination of the bridge's piers. Her heart gave a sudden, painful contraction. There was another horse approaching from the opposite direction. The rider dismounted and began to descend the bank. Amelia could see that the stranger was wearing trousers. Could it be a woman disguised in men's clothing? She heard the figure raise its voice to call Hunter and realized that it was no one but Carter, the estate manager. She was glad that there was no one to see her blush.

There was no doubt in her mind now that his days were indeed full of treks through fields, re-roofing cottages and planning drainage systems. Her relief was tinged with resentment that he preferred these fascinating activities to spending time with her. After all, most gentlemen were content to let their estate manager take care of these things while they went hunting or fishing. She turned the mare toward the Wheelers' house.

On the way home, her path took her past the Dower House, and she was surprised to see that the place was a hive of activity. Hunter's mother must be returning from town sooner than expected. She drew up the mare at the front steps.

"Hello, Watkins. Has the dowager lady Westhaven returned from London?"

"She'll be here tomorrow, milady," the dowager's maid replied. At that moment, a tall young man emerged from the house. When he saw Amelia, his face lit up with an open expression of pleasure.

"My dear Amelia!"

"Thomas, how nice that you are here. I hope your trip was easy."

"Awful. The roads are in a terrible state. It was like trying to drive through trifle all the way here. Mama will be here tomorrow, unless her coach gets stuck in the mud, which it more than likely will. I will stay until she is settled in." Thomas looked very much like his brother, but his face lacked that certain intensity—the driven purposefulness that made Hunter's face look stern when he forgot to smile.

"Oh, I do hope that you will stay for a long while.

Surely you should give the girls of the marriage mart a little time to pine for you." Amelia laughed brightly.

Thomas lifted her down from her mare and insisted that she come in for tea. "You can see all of the 'improvements' Mama ordered to be completed before she moved in. Do you remember what the place used to look like?"

"Vaguely," Amelia admitted, gazing admiringly at the fashionable cream and gold drawing room.

"Mama is bored to flinders by Town. I am delighted to have her out of the way, since she is eternally trying to foist some sweet young thing off on me." He settled Amelia in a gilded crocodile-legged chair and rang for tea. "You must not be anxious on account of her, though. I have insisted that she promise that she will not come to Crownhaven oftener than once a week, and that she will entirely leave the lovebirds to their peace."

"Oh, but I should be delighted to see her more often than that!" Amelia exclaimed, then realized that she sounded a good deal too enthusiastic to see company.

"How polite you are." Thomas's look was penetrating. "Don't tell me that Hunter has been neglecting you already." His voice was light, but there was concern beneath the teasing tone.

"Of course not," she replied curtly, "but he is extremely devoted to the estate."

"Crownhaven is an estate that could practically run itself. Even with this rain, the tenants will do better with their crops than the neighboring lands. The drainage and runoff planning is excellent."

Amelia nodded. "You did a marvelous job running the place when Hunter was in Spain. He just feels a need to become reacquainted with it." She took a sip of tea and tried to convince herself that this was the case.

"Indeed." Thomas sat in thought for a moment.

"Well, you know Hunter better than any of us, Millie. He gets distracted by his notions of obligation. It is hard for him to relax. Sometimes he just needs to be pounced on and reminded to enjoy himself."

"Don't worry," she replied with a cheerfulness she did not feel. "I will remind him. Did you see my family when you were in London?"

"Indeed. I collect that they will be coming home soon. There is hardly anyone left in Town. The season was rather flat this year, as I am sure you will hear from my mother *ad nauseum*. The weather prevented many outdoor events. Vauxhall and such places must have been depressingly soggy indeed."

"My papa will be thrilled to be dragged back from Town. He thinks of nothing but returning to Harrow End from the moment he leaves."

"Yes, I'd say you'll have the whole crowd descending upon you soon enough. You should enjoy your relative solitude while you can." Thomas laughed.

"Indeed, and it will not be long before there is one more added to the crowd."

"Oh, you mean Miriam's child," he grinned sheepishly. "I never know what to do about that. Am I supposed to pretend that I do not know? It is such an awkward thing. But I mean that Jack will be coming back to Harrow End, too."

"Jack? Why? I thought he meant to set up an establishment in Town."

"Well, I daresay he did." Thomas rubbed his chin with a slightly guilty look. "I doubt he would wish me to tell you, but I think he was pretty well in dun territory when I saw him last."

"Oh, dear. Jack always did play deep. Was he too hounded by creditors to stay?" She sighed. "Poor Jack. I think somehow Miriam got all the sense in the family and left Jack and me with nothing at all. I don't know how he will contrive to get out of his fix this time. Papa was livid the last time he had to pay his gaming debts."

"That's what Jack said. I would not have said anything except that I suspect that he will try to cozy up to you with some scheme. Some horse that is guaranteed to win or the usual rot. See that he doesn't gammon you now that you have your portion."

Amelia indulged in a fit of laughter. "You would not be warning me if he had not already gammoned you! I am quite onto all of Jack's schemes. But thank you all the same for your warning. The poor creature will have to marry an heiress at the rate he carries on."

"Well, you may play matchmaker for him. I suspect he will be on a repairing lease to the country for quite some time."

Amelia rose to go. "Thank you, Thomas. You have quite cheered me up. I will drive over to Harrow End tomorrow and assess the damage." She put her hand in his. "Thank you," she said seriously.

"Indeed. I am always happy to amuse you. Come down again when Mama is settled." He walked her out to her horse and helped her to mount. "And remind Hunter what a lucky dog he is," he called out after her.

Nine

She did not have the chance to remind Hunter what a lucky dog he was, Amelia thought bitterly, as the carriage rolled out the drive toward her family's house. He had sent over a message that he would be dining with some neighbors and did not make an appearance in the drawing room where she sat and sewed for hours after dinner. She had heard the floorboards in the hall creak very late when he came up to bed and his low voice through the wall as he dismissed his valet. And then there was silence. She half hoped that he would visit her room, but the adjoining door remained closed. It was strange to think of him lying awake in his bed not far from where she was lying awake in hers. His lamp lit a faint glow beneath the door for hours and was still flickering when she fell asleep at last.

She pressed her gloved hands together and thought about going home. Of course everyone would be delighted to see her, since it had been fully five weeks since she had last seen them at the wedding. She repressed memories of the wedding. Yes, it would be nice now that her family was back at home after the season, and she could go and visit them whenever she wished. Surely between visits to Hunter's mother and her own family, she could stave off some of the terrible loneliness she had felt since coming to Crownhaven.

It was not long before Harrow End came in sight. Amelia felt her insides twist in a painful little dance of happiness. She could see Jack and Miriam come out of the house and she leapt out of the carriage before the steps were down.

"Lady Westhaven. How good of you to visit us." Jack bowed formally over her hand.

Amelia nodded regally and offered the hand to her sister.

"If you think I am going to curtsey and kiss your hand as though you were the royal princess, you had better revise your opinion," Miriam quipped, with a dry smile. She gave a faint scream when Amelia enveloped her in an affection-starved hug.

"Good heavens, Amelia! Conduct yourself!" She rearranged her shawl. "You'll squash the child."

"Hello, Nephew!" Amelia leaned over and called out to her sister's slightly rounded belly.

"You're impossible." Miriam squeezed her sister's hand fondly. "It could be a girl."

"And it looks as though we are only minutes away from finding out," Jack laughed. He ignored his elder sister as she protested indignantly that she was only now beginning to show. "Mama will be so glad that you have come," he continued as he ushered his sisters inside. "Where is your big brute of a husband, Millie?"

Amelia cringed inwardly. "He was so sorry that he could not accompany me," she said lightly, "but we had a bit of an emergency with one of the tenant's cottages. Westhaven is renovating nearly all of them."

"Pity. I have hardly seen him since he returned. You stole him away instantly, you minx. Mama, here is the prodigal daughter returned."

Lady Harrow embraced her daughter and then held her out at arm's length. "You look blooming, my dear," she pronounced, but there was a faint expression of worry in her eyes. She ordered tea and then swept her children into the drawing room. She helped settle Miriam on the settee, but her eyes were on her youngest child. "How is Westhaven?" she asked pointedly.

Amelia spun out her lie with a vague shrug of her shoulders. It was hard to sit there and tell them how happy they were and how much he regretted that he was not able to call upon them. She had not even told him that she was driving to Harrow End. It wasn't as though he would care.

Everyone seemed to accept her story easily enough and instantly launched into the various *on dit* that had shocked, amused, or annoyed the *ton* for the rest of the season.

"I must say, I was glad to have it all end this year. It was getting to be too much for me, and Miriam has not been in any state to go out in public for the last three weeks at least. Your father was desperate to get home again, but I thought that we might be crowding you if we came back too soon." Her mother patted her knee.

"I knew that as soon as we returned you would feel obliged to spend time with us, and I wanted to leave you two alone," she continued. "What a pity you couldn't do a proper honeymoon tour on the Continent. Perhaps Westhaven should have considered America. Or India . . . And then when I heard that Lady Westhaven, the dowager Lady Westhaven, I mean, was coming back to Bedfordshire, well, there was no reason for us to stay from home. . . . Well, here is your father now."

Amelia ran to her father and kissed him. He lumbered over to a chair and sat down looking uncomfortable. "Poor Papa. I should have come out to you in the stables. I know how you hate visiting in the drawing room."

"Demmed silly acting as though you were a guest," he agreed.

"Clement! You might come out of the stables to see your own daughter! I swear you would take your meals there if I let you."

Amelia looked around the room as her family laughed and quarreled as they always did. The yellow brocade of the wall hangings, the portraits on these walls, the pianoforte sitting next to the harp in the corner. . . . They were all just as they were when she left for London to marry Westhaven. Oh, it seemed like years ago. She blinked away the sting behind her eyes. There was no purpose in wishing she had never married him. She was a complete baby to be feeling so sentimental.

Her mother moved over to sit beside her under the cover of an argument between Jack and her father regarding the paces of the bays that had carried off young Miss Wellham to marry her secret beau at Gretna Green.

"You look a little peaked, my dear." Lady Harrow looked at her intently. "Is it possible that you are . . . in a delicate situation?"

Amelia laughed bitterly and refrained from telling her that she was in a distinctly uncomfortable situation. "No, I don't believe so, Mama."

"But you might be?" she pressed.

"Expecting? I—I suppose I might be. But I don't think so." Surely not.

Her mother squeezed her arm. "Well, if you find that you are, tell me first thing. I will be right over to take care of you. Miriam will be confined in another three months, and it will be just the thing for me to help her look after the baby and at the same time, you can learn a thing or two about caring for infants. I do hope you will not be offended that Miriam wants to take Nurse with her when Lord Wells comes back. She has been living with her sister, but Miriam has persuaded her to come out of retirement to care for the babe. We shall find you another nurse."

"Of course," Amelia replied vaguely, overwhelmed by the tide of her mother's ramblings.

"I say, Millie, do come out and take a turn in the garden with me. I have a few questions I would like to ask you about Crownhaven." Jack jumped to his feet with a good deal too much enthusiasm and offered his sister his arm.

Amelia allowed him to lead her into the garden with some anxiety. "What is it that you want, Jack. Why are you up from Town? I do hope that you are not on one of your 'repairing leases.' "

"Afraid so, Milzie. Gad, but it is a fine day. It is about time we had a fine day after all this rain. It rained five days out of seven last week. You would think that the odds would be against it, but so it did. Lost ten pounds on it."

"So you are in debt again?"

Jack looked sheepish. "Don't put on that Miriam face. I am a bit dipped if you must know. I just needed a bit of time off for my luck to turn."

"Creditors dunning you, I suppose." She sighed resignedly.

"A bit. But you see, Millie, that is just what I wanted to talk to you about. I have a grand scheme that will keep me flush for the rest of my days."

"Whatever it is, no," she said resolutely.

"But you see, it is a sure thing. I have it on oath that Katie Gee will place at the next meet."

"No."

"I was thinking," he continued doggedly, "since you are now in possession of your portion . . ."

"Jack, no! You know I cannot touch that money without Hunter's approval." She looked at him sternly.

"And he would not approve. Neither do I. You simply must learn to practice some economy."

"But it is a sure thing!" he protested. "It is really more of an investment than a loan, you see. You will get back more than what you give me."

"Jack, it is always the same story with you. Do what you always do: enjoy your time here, plague Miriam, wheedle Papa out of the money, and go off to Town to back your sure thing."

"You are turning into Miriam," he teased. "I didn't have too much hope that you would come through for me. Do you think Hunter would?"

"No."

Jack shrugged. "Not a whit of enterprise in that man."

"Not a whit," she agreed cheerfully.

She had been so happy to see them she thought that it would be agony when the visit was over. But as her carriage rolled down the drive into the late summer dusk, she admitted that she was happy to be leaving them as well. It was too much activity after too much solitude. As much as she did not want to admit it, and as much as she loved its occupants, Harrow End was no longer her home.

"I thought I should find you here."

Hunter looked up from the remains of his luncheon. "Thomas! Amelia said you were here. Getting the Dower House ready for Mama, I suppose. When will she come?" He rose to his feet and shook his brother warmly by the hand.

Thomas led his mount to the fallen tree where his brother's horse was tied and wrapped the reins around a branch. "Tomorrow," he replied with a shrug. He stood for a moment looking over the smooth surface of the lake. "You always used to come here after one of Father's tantrums. Not a whimper, even when he beat you, but you always escaped here afterward. You used to say it helped you to forget." He flung himself onto the grass beside Hunter. "What are you trying to forget now?"

Hunter gave an uncomfortable laugh and idly dug the heels of his riding boots into the soft ground. "It just seemed like a nice place to eat lunch on the first fine day we've had in a fortnight." Amelia must have told him how he had been treating her. He felt an annoying wash of shame to be taken to task by his brother.

Thomas snorted his disbelief. "You have only been back from Spain three months, and it must seem like the whole world has changed since you went away. I think perhaps it would have been wiser to postpone your wedding until you were more . . . adjusted."

"I was promised to Amelia. I was not about to cry off," he growled menacingly.

"I never suggested you would cry off," his brother replied calmly. "Hunter, have you seen yourself lately? It's not just England that's changed—it's you. You disappear for days in London, you walk off in the middle of conversations, you pace incessantly. Don't look at me like that—you know it is true."

He felt the familiar pressure in his chest and resisted the urge to get up and pace. "So what if it is true. This is the new me. Everyone will just have to get used to it!" He viciously tore off a piece of bread and threw it into the pond where a family of ducks quarreled cheerfully over it.

"You seem very unhappy."

He clenched his jaw. Tom was beginning to sound like Amelia. Why was everyone so insistent upon invading his psyche? He pressed his fingers to his eyes for a moment and sighed. "I am unhappy because everyone is always pestering me as to why I am unhappy. My very presence brings a cloud of gloom over everyone in the room. I am sure Amelia ran crying to you to tell you what a monster I have become." From the corner of his eye he saw his brother's head snap around to look at him, but he continued to stare at the water in front of him.

"Amelia said you two could not be happier."

"She lied."

"But she did not betray the state your marriage is in. She is a very loyal creature, your wife."

"She shouldn't be my wife. I should have released her from the engagement long ago. I can't make her happy. I can't even stand to be around her. She should have married you."

Thomas took some of the bread and threw pieces on the bank to entice the ducks out of the water. "She never would have. It's you she loves."

Hunter made an expression of disgust. "She doesn't love me. She worships me. She thinks I am some kind of god. Some glorious hero who will fulfill her every dream." He ran a claw-like hand savagely through his hair. "It doomed me to failure from the start." He narrowed his eyes as he looked across the lake. When he next spoke his voice sounded bitter, even to himself. "You should have seen her on our wedding night. Horror, Thomas. She looked at me with horror. The idol had tumbled. She can't even bring herself to kiss me now." He gave a humorless laugh. "As if you wished to know these things."

He thought of the day in the cottage. He had behaved like an animal. He had bedded her like a lightskirt on the floor. She must have been so humiliated. Yes, she had enjoyed it—obviously they both had. It was afterward, when the familiar panic descended on his chest, when he felt himself mentally withdrawing from her after that intense physical and emotional intimacy, that she must have felt used. He had seen the hurt expression on her face before he turned away to put on his clothes and pace out the restless, hunted feeling that had overwhelmed him.

They watched the ducks lumber gracelessly across the grass. "I think," Thomas said at last, "that Amelia would be perfectly happy with you if you were happy with yourself."

"Thank you, O Oracle."

His brother gave a good-natured laugh, but did not excuse himself.

"Yes," Hunter admitted in annoyance. "I suppose I feel guilty for leaving the regiment and guilty for not being all that Amelia has set me up to be. She wants to know everything about me—what I'm thinking, what I'm feeling all the time." He rubbed his forehead in frustration and resignedly threw the rest of his lunch to the pleading ducks. "I am an unfeeling brute, I know, but I cannot stand her prying into my emotions all the time."

"I imagine she just feels distanced from you," Thomas replied. "We all do. You have closed yourself off in a way we cannot understand."

He felt the anger rise in him. "No one can understand! I come back to England to find that life has gone on without me and the *ton* could care less about the men in Spain. Some chit at the betrothal ball asked me who this Ciudad-Rodrigo fellow was and was he dead yet." He found his rage was replaced with disgust. "Half the world has no idea what happened to me and my men in Spain and the other half wants to climb inside my head and make me explain it all." Hunter rose and brushed off his breeches. "Well"—he tapped himself on the chest—"there is little wonder I seem changed."

With a tight smile of angry self-mockery, he swept up his coat and strode off to his horse.

It was pouring rain again the next day. Amelia was beginning to expect to hear the drumroll of it on her window in the morning. She lay in bed, wondering vaguely if Jack had bet for, or against, the downpour. He had most likely staked his last shilling that the sun would be splitting the stones today.

Sarah had said that the dowager arrived that morning. She should visit her mother-in-law and welcome her back to Crownhaven. Another visit trying to explain why Hunter had not accompanied her.

It had been very provoking yesterday to have to pretend to her family that everything was perfectly affable between her and her husband. Especially when he didn't appreciate it. She entertained a vision of her entire family storming Crownhaven when they heard how Hunter neglected her. The thought of Miriam, vastly pregnant and uttering war whoops, was highly pleasing.

She rang for Sarah and began dragging a brush through her hair. Did Hunter actually neglect her? More than likely, he spent as much time with her as most husbands did with their wives. He had always been pleasant, and he had visited her bedchamber regularly. No, he was likely behaving with perfect husbandry propriety. It was she who was expecting too much.

"Sarah, could you bring down a carriage dress? I think I shall go and pay a visit on the dowager Lady Westhaven."

"In this weather, milady?" Sarah gasped.

Amelia crossed to the window and watched the rain pour down for a moment. "Yes," she said at last, "I think I will brave it after all." Sarah went to find a suitable gown, murmuring only slightly inaudibly about chills and death.

What of Miriam and Lord Wells? Amelia sipped her chocolate and paced the room. Their marriage was based only on proper respect and admiration. And then Wells left for Jamaica even when there was a baby on the way. That was hardly a romantic way to behave. Yes, she was acting like a ninny. Her husband was treating her no differently than any other husband treated his wife. *Love is vulgar,* she reminded herself. *Gently bred people do not succumb to any excess of emotion.* She pressed back the fervent wish that she had been born a merchant's daughter.

It was indeed a good deal too wet to go visiting, but she put on her oilskin cloak, ordered the closed carriage, and, to Coachman John's disgust, continued in her determination to pay a visit on the dowager.

"Why, Lady Westhaven!" that lady exclaimed with great surprise, just as though the butler had not announced who had come to call.

"Please, do call me Amelia like you used to do, ma'am," Amelia begged as she took her mother-in-law's hands.

"Of course. And you must call me the Dowager Lady Westhaven. Or Mama, if you prefer. Though I doubt you would, as you have a perfectly good Mama of your own. Yes, you should call me the dowager to remind me that that is what I am now."

Amelia's noise of protest went unheard. "Would you like some tea? I am sure that ours is not as good as that at Crownhaven." The dowager raised her thin brows in a slightly pained expression and rang for the butler.

"We drink the same blend from Fortnum and Mason as you do, ma'am," Amelia reminded her.

"Well, I do hope that you lock it up. I have long suspected that Wedgeworth and Mrs. Egan are stealing it." Hunter's mother frowned. She looked around the sumptuous drawing room in disdain. "How are you enjoying living in my house? I mean Crownhaven, of course. I simply must be reminded that it is not my house anymore."

Amelia stirred sugar into her tea with deliberate slowness before replying. "It is lovely. I have loved it from my childhood. You have kept the place in impeccable order."

"Thank you, Lady Westhaven." The dowager sighed heavily and reached for the clotted cream. "And now I shall have to begin again in this drafty old barn."

"You must come over to Crownhaven whenever you like."

"Indeed, I think that that would make me quite blue deviled. Of course that is the natural order of things. I suppose you shall be shuffled out here to die one day, too." She raised her eyes to the beautifully corniced ceiling and sighed again. "Why has my son not come with you?" she asked at last, turning her eyes back to Amelia.

"He—He had to meet with Carter."

"Carter will ruin us. That man was always out to skim off the top. Thomas always had to watch him like a hawk when I lived at Crownhaven."

"I think that Hunter has every confidence in him. He has been the estate manager for ten years at least."

"And stealing from us as long," the dowager snorted. "These scones are not at all good." She examined the untasted one on her plate with distaste. "I am of the definite opinion that Cook drinks."

"I think they are delicious," Amelia volunteered.

"They don't look quite right. I daresay Hunter will come to see me tomorrow. Perhaps he wanted to see me alone. I do hope his shoulder has improved. It was terrible to see him injured. I could barely stand to look at him."

"It has improved a good deal. He has nearly all his strength back."

"I shall reserve my judgment until I have seen him myself, Lady Westhaven. There are some things only a mother knows. Spain was not at all good for his constitution. I hardly knew him when he returned."

"I did not either!" Amelia exclaimed, feeling a sudden wash of camaraderie. "He is so changed. He seems so distracted these days. He blames himself for the men who lost their lives there."

The dowager's brows rose in disdain. "Well, I do hope you are not plaguing the life out of him. You'll very likely make matters worse. Men marry for heirs and for someone to have a pleasant conversation with after dinner. I shouldn't have thought that I would have to tell you these things, Lady Westhaven, but indeed, if you were doing your duty in either of those areas . . . well, perhaps I should send over some recipes to your cook. A nice meal like he used to get when I lived at Crownhaven will no doubt improve his spirits. Of course I would send my own cook, but he is simply unreliable. I shall have to discharge him, whether he's French or not."

"You are very kind, ma'am," Amelia managed between clenched teeth. "I am certain that Hunter will be over to welcome you back as soon as he possibly can." She rose to depart.

"I am sorry that you missed Thomas. He left this morning on a week's grouse shooting in Scotland. He was supposed to help me settle in here, but he's off already. I really think he only said he would accompany me because it was on his way. But of course I was never one to interfere with the pleasures of my children." She rose to her feet and gravely shook hands with her daughter-in-law. "Do forgive me for not seeing you out. The draft in the hallway is terrible. I suspect I will not last the winter what with the wind blowing through every crack in this place." The dowager bowed her out and then settled herself again on her chaise before the cozy fire.

Amelia shrugged off her annoyance as she climbed into the coach. It was too bad she could not discuss Hunter's malady with his mother. She resolved to ask the advice of Dr. Sterling. Perhaps her husband's restlessness stemmed from his injury. It had healed well, but it was possible that such a shock to the system had long-lasting effects on the nerves. She remembered how happy he had been as they bivouacked in the little cottage, and she felt an ache of longing for him.

Her ruminations were cut short with a jolt that nearly flung her to the floor. The right front wheel of the carriage had dropped into a deep rut and the horses could not pull it out. Over the drum of the rain she could hear the coachman swearing as the animals slipped and strained in the mud. The rocking of the coach only served to settle it more firmly in the mired road. After a quarter hour of struggling, John gave up and opened the carriage door.

"I'm sorry, milady. They can't pull it out," he panted, the rain streaming off his oilskin. "We're only a half mile from the house. If you don't mind waiting, I'll go bring back some help. It will only take a few minutes." He seemed to take this event as a personal failing, so Amelia assured him fulsomely that she was quite comfortable and sat back to wait.

Ten

The extreme tilt of the carriage afforded her an interesting perspective, and she was watching the water sluice down the road as though it were a riverbed when the door was flung open.

"Hunter!" She was quite unprepared to face her husband.

He did not reply, but put out a damp glove and indicated that she should climb out. She awkwardly struggled up the sloping floor of the coach. "The carriage is stuck," she announced unnecessarily.

A ghost of a smile crossed his face "Why so it is." He looked very dashing on his big roan, with his oilskins black with rain and water running off his hat. The injured angle of the vehicle was such that he had not needed to dismount in order to be on the same level as her. He took her around the waist and transferred her in one motion from the coach to a position before him on his horse.

"Why did you go out on a day like this?" he chided softly.

"I went to see your mother," she replied. She watched the men empty bags of sand under the wheel of the carriage and did not turn her face up to him.

He enveloped her with his cloak. His chest against her back was warm. She tried not to think about it.

"What a widgeon you are. You should have waited until the weather was better." His arm around her waist was very distracting. "Besides, you have now made me look to be a terrible son."

"Indeed, no. She informed me that you would be over to see her tomorrow," she replied slyly.

He exhaled an exaggerated sigh of disgust onto the back of her neck. "Did she? Now I shall have to ride over, even if it is raining hailstones as big as my fist."

"Of course you will. And she is going to send you home with some recipes for me to give to Cook. She is convinced that food nostalgia is at the root of your doldrums."

"Amelia," he said suddenly into her hair, "I am sorry. I have been an unfeeling monster in the past weeks."

Amelia looked up at him at last. "You are the one who has been unhappy. Why?"

"I don't know." He looked down at her rain-freckled face. "But please don't give up on me. I need you. I need you to remind me that the world is good." His mouth twisted up in a tentative smile.

"The world *is* good. I don't know why you insist on making things so difficult," she said frankly.

He frowned, his brows nearly meeting each other. "I just feel as though I left things . . . unfinished in Spain."

"Well," she said, "I suppose you left the war unfinished. But that was hardly your fault."

"I know." He seemed to fidget behind her on the roan. "There is just so much . . . well, there is no point in talking about it." His arm around her tightened. "Don't give up on me yet, my dear." There was a huskiness to his jovial words.

She relaxed against him at last, and he urged the horse toward the house. "I love you so much, Hunter. Please don't push me away."

He pressed a passionate kiss into her hair. "I am the most fortunate man in the world to be loved by such a woman as you."

Amelia felt his words warm her. It was almost as though he had said he loved her. They arrived at the front door of Crownhaven sooner than she would have liked. "How ridiculous that you would have to rescue me," she laughed, as he lifted her down from the roan. "I could easily walk to the Dower House in fine weather, and we were already almost halfway back when the carriage got stuck. I could have practically shouted for help from the stables."

"You must allow me to be heroic on some occasions." He kept his hands around her waist and looked down at her.

Amelia twined her arms around his neck and tilted her head back to look at him. His short military-cropped hair had grown so much that dark, wet strands fell over his forehead and dripped in his eyes.

"Will I take him to the stables, milord?" the groom asked pointedly.

"Yes, yes, of course." Hunter waved him away with a sheepish grin. "How gauche of us to engage in such an affectionate embrace in front of the servants. I will never be respected here again."

"Yes, and they will think that you do not have any sense, if you don't come in out of the rain." She took him by the hand and led him inside.

If Wedgeworth felt any dismay at the small ornamental lake forming in the marble hallway around the embracing form of his employers, he refrained from expressing it until he was belowstairs. Hunter cheerfully disentangled himself, ordered tea in the library, ordered his wife upstairs to change, and went whistling up to his rooms in a better mood than his household had seen since his return.

Amelia toweled her hair dry and tried in vain to restore its former waves. Her curls were turning frizzy with the damp, so she scraped them back into a smooth chignon and changed into a long-sleeved plum-colored gown. She felt like dancing as Sarah helped her into it. Hunter loved her! If he had not said as much, she could feel it in his embrace. She could see it in the endless depths of his dark eyes. They would start again. It would be a marriage like she had dreamed about in the long years that he was gone.

Hunter was in the library when she arrived. He looked as though he had never been outside, except for the damp hair that clung to his temples. It made him look almost boyish. She seated herself in a chair by the fire and took the glass of ratafia he offered.

"I decided that you needed something stronger than tea."

She watched in amusement as he poured himself a glass. "You like ratafia? It hardly seems like a soldier's drink."

He regarded the glass with scorn. "I think I would prefer claret. But perhaps you would as well." He crossed the room to the decanter. "My mother always offered ladies ratafia when they needed something stronger than tea. It seemed like the thing to do. For all I know, you simply adore gin.

She laughed. "I shall take the ratafia. Though you are correct. I have no idea why it seems to be ladylike." She sipped meditatively. "Perhaps I would like gin. I was never offered it."

"I am certain that I can oblige you. But it is definitely a cultivated taste."

"No, thank you." She wrinkled her nose in distaste. "I suppose I should be thankful that you do not have vices like drinking or gambling or going to those horrid mills where men beat each other half to death."

He pulled her up from her chair, seated himself, and dragged her onto his lap. "No, my vices consist of ignoring you," he said ruefully.

"Nonsense. I will not hear such libel of my husband." She laughed. It was wonderful to be so close to him. She drew in a deep breath; there was something about him that smelled so nice. "Your mother appears to be in good health," she commented, trying not to think about the day in the cottage.

"Is she? She sounds to be in fine fighting form."

"She has changed a great many things about the Dower House. It is quite the first stare of fashion now."

"I suspected as much. I am sure she told you exactly how you should be running Crownhaven, told you how to keep 'her' silver and plate, and insisted that the servants were stealing tea."

Amelia laughed again and returned to the chair. "Something like that."

"I know her. Don't you let her bully you. You are mistress here now and that is exactly how things should be. If she gets too out of hand, ask her what it was like when she married Papa and my grandmama moved to the Dower House. Oh, you should have heard the squalls then. I always thought that the fourth Lord Westhaven should have built the Dower House much farther away from the main house. Perhaps in Yorkshire . . ."

"Well, I don't blame her for feeling put out at having to move out of this beautiful place." She looked appreciatively around the library with its mahogany bookcases and high ceiling. "Your mother is so proud of you. You should have heard her talk about you while you were gone. She was almost as incessant as me. Each of us used to subtly gloat whenever we got a letter from you and the other didn't."

"I had no idea I sponsored such a delightful pastime between mother and daughter-in-law. And you said mills are barbaric. . . ." He smiled with one side of his mouth.

Amelia's insides went tight. How was it that they had been married nearly six weeks, and he still had the power to weaken her with a smile?

"You saw Thomas today?" Hunter continued.

"No, he has gone up to Scotland for the grouse."

"Now if there is anyone with a right to feel displaced, it is he." Hunter's voice was low.

"What do you mean?"

"Thomas had the run of everything while I was gone and then, bang, when I return he is expected to drop graciously back into the role of younger brother."

"He didn't mind," Amelia insisted kindly.

"I would have if I were him. He was expected to keep the whole estate shipshape for me, knowing that he would never inherit it. I'll wager he wished heartily for my death a score of times." He sighed.

"Hunter! How can you be so morose? Thomas seems perfectly happy to have you running Crownhaven again. I don't think any resentment ever entered his head. You know how good-natured he is."

There was a long silence in which Hunter twirled the stem of the glass between his fingers. "Of course," he said at last. "You are right. I am only thinking of how I would feel if I were him." His brows drew together. "There are times when I think how much better it would have been for everyone if I had died in Spain." He gave a dry laugh. "It seems like a mistake of fate that I survived to come and live out my privileged life in England while so many more honorable, brave, talented men did not. Men who were needed."

"I will not hear you say this," Amelia said sharply, sitting up straighter in her chair. "I need you. Your family needs you. Your children will need you. You will never, ever say those things, or even think those things again. I don't know why you lived through it when others did not; I was not in charge of deciding. It was not a matter of deserving it or not. You cannot go on feeling guilty for living. I am sure you would have felt very sorry for yourself if you had died."

He looked at her blankly at this ridiculous statement and then a rueful smile curved his mouth. "Yes, I probably would have," he said slowly.

"Now listen to me, Major. I am commanding you now." She cocked a stern eyebrow at him. "You are to get on to the business of living. You will take your wife for drives, you will take her to the assembly at Kempston, and you will dance three full dances with her, including"—she kicked his leg gently with her slippered foot—"the supper dance. You will begin drawing again, and on the next fine day you will take her to Bleighford Abbey for a picturesque, artistic, sort of day." She waved her hand vaguely.

He gave her a mock salute. "Yes, commander."

Hunter lay in the grass and chewed idly on a piece of grass. The sky was blue for the first time in a week. He watched as enormous wads of clouds slowly expanded and collapsed. The afternoon must be waning; the clouds were beginning to be tinted with pink on their western faces. It was a bit like the sky in the Sistine Chapel. Only less populated with scantily clad foundlings.

He had received a letter from his solicitor that morning, before they had set out on the promised picnic to Bleighford Abbey. Roberts had located several of the families of the men in his company. It was up to him to decide if he wanted to contact them. It was a difficult decision. It would be agonizing to rake up those memories, when he wanted nothing better than to put Spain behind him. But perhaps this was the only way to accomplish that.

The face of his wife loomed suddenly over him.

"Are you still so hungry after that enormous luncheon that Cook sent with us that you are eating grass?" she teased. "Perhaps you can have these for dessert." She laid a bunch of wildflowers on his chest.

"It is you I am hungry for." He narrowed his eyes predatorily. He swept the arm she leaned on out from under her, and she collapsed into an untidy heap beside him.

"What a ridiculous thing to say," she laughed. "You sound like a stage villain."

"Forget your lover—run away with me," he growled with a bad Italian accent. He rolled onto his elbow and drew her closer.

"You are crushing my flowers."

He extracted the mangled bouquet from between them. "I don't know why you care about these when you have a thousand hothouse blooms at home," he muttered.

"Hunter," she said in a changed voice, "do you remember that day . . . in the cottage?" She turned her face away, but he could see her ear growing pink.

He felt a strange rush of tenderness toward that pink ear. "Of course. How could I forget?" He tickled her averted cheek with a daisy.

"Why was it so awkward afterward? I felt as though you disapproved."

"No, Millie, that was not it at all. I'm sorry that you should have thought that." He took her chin and gently forced her to look at him. "I am always pleased to have your . . . ah . . . amorous attention."

"Is passion so very ungenteel that we cannot indulge in it when we are alone?" she asked, a tiny furrow forming on her forehead.

"No, no, it is not that." He lay silent for a moment, twining the flowers she had picked into a daisy chain. "I don't know," he said at last. "Perhaps it is that. I suppose that I felt that you endured . . . my. . . .your . . . marital duties and that any excess of . . . passion or lust or whatever you want to call it would be repulsive to you." He broke the head off a primrose. "Damn it all, Millie, I find it hard to talk of these things to you." He rolled away from her feeling ashamed.

He felt her hand on his back. "I wish you did not." She leaned her cheek on his shoulder and he felt her hair brush his cheek. It smelled nice, like lavender. "I do not find your attentions in the least bit repulsive, Hunter. You have taught me that the 'marital duties' as you call them, can be very pleasant indeed."

He continued plaiting the flower stems together, willing her not to move from him. It was novel to be comforted by human contact. "I was always taught that lust was reserved for lightskirts and mistresses, and that such an eagerness to couple should never be shown a wife. It is disrespectful." He frowned when he heard her laugh.

"You make it sound so funny. 'Eagerness to couple.' What a silly expression." She put her head back down on the grass so that she could look up at him. "I don't think that it is disrespectful. I would find it flattering. It would make me feel attractive."

"Attractive? Millie, you are beautiful! I could not believe how lovely you had grown when I saw you the first day I returned." He was rewarded by her blush. "I am very pleased with you, Lady Westhaven. I shall do my best to refrain from showing you respect in the future." He shot her a wicked look.

"Please do. I can't abide respect," she laughed.

"Excellent." He put the crown of flowers he had fashioned onto her head.

"Hunter?" Her face was ludicrously serious beneath the garland that dipped low over one eye. "When we do . . . make love . . . would you stay with me for a while afterward?"

He touched her cheek gently, wishing he could brush off the blush that accompanied her request. "I would like that," he said at last, his voice soft. "I give you my word that I will no longer respect you, and once I am finished not respecting you, I will bore you with long monologues late into the night." He leaned low over her body and laughed. "I will show you."

She did not mistake his intentions. "Now?" she exclaimed breathlessly.

"Why not?" He began a slow exploration of the region behind her ear.

Her laugh was low and sensual. "Why is it that you always seem to feel passionate out of doors?"

"Now that I have your permission, my dear, I think I shall feel it in any number of random places." He heard her draw in her breath sharply as he bared her shoulder. "The back garden . . . linen closet . . . the pianoforte." He was not sure she was paying attention to what he was saying, but her back arched in response to his caress. He stopped talking.

Eleven

They rode back sitting pressed together in the driving seat of the old carriage. Amelia still wore the garland he had made for her, though its wilted blooms threatened to come apart with every jog of the carriage.

"It is so nice to spend time with you," she sighed, leaning her cheek on his sleeve.

He made a noise of assent.

"We will be so happy. I want nothing more than to make you happy. I would do anything for you. You know that, don't you?"

Hunter physically restrained himself from pulling away from her. He could feel the unwelcome, yet familiar rush of anxiety. What was wrong with him? Why could she not be like other people's wives? Why did she have to cling to him? There was an unpleasant responsibility in being the sole source of someone else's happiness. He felt itchy all over.

"Hunter?" He realized that she had been trying to get his attention for several minutes.

"Yes?" His eyes roamed her face. The darkness of her curls set off her fair complexion in a way that made her appear almost fragile.

"You are doing it again."

"Doing what?"

"You are pulling away from me. Why?"

"Don't be silly." He put an arm around her to demonstrate his closeness.

Her expression was perplexed. "You said you wouldn't, but you are."

"What? What are you talking about?" His voice was harsher than he had meant it to be.

"Why won't you let me get close to you? Why won't you let me love you?"

"I am close to you!" He chose not to address the second question.

"You know what I mean."

"Amelia, what more do you want from me? I have spent the day with you. We have made love outside after a picnic lunch. What is it that you want?" Blast it but the afternoon had become unpleasantly hot.

"You have not spoken to me since we . . ."

"You are being entirely unreasonable. I have far too many things to do than to waste my time dancing attendance on you if you are going to constantly demand more from me. I refuse to live in your pocket." He hated the way he sounded. But he was possessed with the urgent need to get away from her. The air was thick with humidity. He could see it hanging like a fog over the fields. Crownhaven was enveloped in a hazy halo at the crest of the next hill. He wished they were there now. The library would be cool and dark. He fixed his eyes on the house and concentrated fully on pushing on toward it. The horse gave a grunt and waddled into a trot when he snapped the whip at her ear. Yes, another half hour and he would be there, safe.

Amelia felt her spine stiffen in disbelief. He was rejecting her again. Even after they had talked about it. Every time she thought she understood him and felt as though she was beginning to get closer to him, he shut himself off. An unpleasant thought occurred to her.

"Hunter," she began in a cool voice, "do you remember the day that you asked me to marry you?"

"Of course," he replied, with some surprise.

"I was in the garden at Harrow End after you had come over to take your leave of us before you went to Spain. I thought you had left, but you rode back and found me and asked me if I wanted to marry you when you came back."

"Yes." He did not offer any further commentary.

"Do you remember what your exact words were?"

Hunter's glance held a look somewhat akin to panic. "Well, I just . . . I said, 'Millie, I would be honored if you would consent to be my wife when I come back from Spain.' I don't remember my exact words."

Amelia gave him a steady look. "You said, 'If you want it, I could marry you if I come back alive from this.' And then you said, 'But don't wait for me, Millie; if you get another offer, take it, because I don't know what is going to happen in Spain.' "

His gaze roved around the countryside as though he were looking for a hiding place. "I said something like that I suppose. Why are you asking such foolish questions?" He made a great pretense of urging the old carriage horse on to a faster amble and then scanned the horizon with great interest.

She lifted her shoulders and let them fall with a sigh. The air was hot and felt as though it had been breathed and exhaled more than a few times over. Midges, spawned in the boggy ditches that bordered the road, hung densely in the humid air. She found herself wishing briefly that it would rain again.

"You did not expect to return from Spain, did you." It was more of a statement than a question. She was hardly aware of having spoken aloud. Her words were not an accusation, just a sudden, sad realization.

There was a long pause. "No."

It hardly mattered that he had answered; she knew that it was true.

"Why did you marry me?"

"Millie, don't take it that way. You know that I am fond of you, and our families feel that this is a good match. It wasn't as though I was going to marry anyone else. This will work out fine." He smiled and tapped her under the chin playfully. "Don't spoil a perfectly nice day with too much talking. We've settled everything, have we not? Now, be a good girl."

"And what?" Amelia asked, with a slight arch of her brows. "And be silent?" She noted the look of surprise in Hunter's dark eyes at the edge to her tone, but did not stop. "I feel very much as though you have tricked me, Lord Westhaven."

"Millie, stop doing this." This must be the voice he used when he commanded the Light Dragoons.

"I will not. You knew how I worshiped you. You let me love you. You let me love you for *three years* while you were trying to get yourself killed in Spain. Everyone in the country thinks that you are a hero, Hunter, but I know you to be a coward. Rather than tell me you didn't care for me, rather than not propose at all, you just left and hoped for the best." She clenched her fists hard in her lap. "Nothing would have pleased you more than if I had married someone else while you were gone."

"I am not going to participate in this histrionic conversation." Hunter drew himself up stiffly and fixed his gaze between the horses' ears.

"Why did you ask me to marry you?" she pressed.

He turned on her, his dark eyes blazing. "I felt sorry for you. I thought it would please you."

Amelia could think of no suitable reply.

* * *

He felt sorry for her. Up in her rooms, she began to struggle out of her grass-stained gown as she tried to quell the nausea that threatened to overwhelm her. Well it was out at last. How pathetic she must look to him. *Oh, Hunter, I want nothing more than to make you happy.* Her mental voice mocked her. Hunter did not wish to be made happy. He wanted to live in his own bleak world full of regrets and guilt. There was no room for her in it.

Fine. She kicked the dress away. It was her own fault. While he was away she had built him up into an imaginary hero. In her mind he was sensitive and strong. He was intelligent and caring. He was . . . well, flat. She sat down at her dressing table in her chemise. The Hunter in her dreams was as two-dimensional as a paper doll. The man she was married to was much more complex.

"Feh," she said aloud to her reflection. "They are his problems." From now on, her life was her own. She would not live to make him happy. She would live to make herself happy.

She kicked off her shoes and padded over to the clothespress to choose a dress for dinner. Inside, her hands found the soft folds of her blue-and-silver wedding gown. She would have to ask Sarah to take it upstairs to be stored. There was no occasion for such a fine dress here in the country. She smoothed the silver tissue of the Illusion Gown with a sigh. So much had happened since she put it on . . . was it really only six weeks? The Illusion Gown indeed.

Amelia looked up in astonishment when Hunter entered the breakfast room. "How kind of you to join me," she said coolly. "I know how you like to get out and go riding early in the morning." She poured him a cup of tea, but then turned back to her breakfast.

He stood awkwardly in the doorway for a moment before he finally came in and took a seat at the table.

Watching him warily, Amelia noticed that he did not take any food from the sideboard. The silence between them was grating on her nerves, but she was too angry with him to do anything to make him more comfortable. Besides, he probably had not even noticed that they had spent the last seven minutes conversationless.

"I'm afraid that I must go to London," he said slowly.

"What? Why?"

"Business. I told you I was thinking of taking my seat in the Lords."

"Yes, but it is in the middle of the session. There is no need to start until next spring." The muffin she was eating suddenly seemed very unappetizing.

"There are other things I need to take care of in Town." He kept his eyes on his empty plate.

"How long will you be gone?" It pained her that he did not offer to take her with him.

"Not above a few weeks. You will have my mother and your family to keep you company." He spoke lightly, but the crease between his brows deepened. "Don't cry."

"I am not crying," she replied with mild surprise, her expression resolutely calm. She noted with vague pleasure that his brows rose slightly. "When will you leave?"

"Tomorrow."

Amelia's eyes flickered to his. His brows were drawn in the straight line that she had come to dread. She applied herself to the breakfast she could no longer taste. "Have a pleasant journey," she said at last with an overbright smile.

Hunter took a hurried gulp of his coffee.

"Well, I must be off. There is a good deal to see to before I go." He did not meet her eyes as he gave her a bow and left the room. The room seemed unnaturally quiet without him. The sunlight was still streaming through the windows and the sparrows outside were still quarreling cheerfully. Amelia dropped her fork and looked at her plate with disgust.

She stabbed her needle into the embroidery frame and jerked the floss savagely through the canvas. It formed an ugly, floppy knot at the front, but she continued her vicious jabs. His good-bye had been relieved from awkwardness only by its brevity. He had pretended a great rush, promised vaguely to write, kissed her on the forehead, and leapt into the coach without ever meeting her eyes.

"Spring 'em!" he had called out to the coachman to preserve the illusion of urgency.

The coach lurched as the coachman gave the animals their heads and started down the gravel drive.

"Coward!" she had screamed out when she knew he was out of hearing. "Coward!" Not even the footmen had looked back. He had run away and left her screaming like a fishmonger's wife on the steps of the house.

She pulled so hard at the floss that it broke. Well, he was a coward, she thought, as she poked blindly at the eye of the needle with a new bit of floss. He was running away to London because he could not stand intimacy. He was a hero in the face of danger but a complete ninny when it came to personal relationships. The floss had frayed and was refusing to thread through the needle. She dropped her hands to her lap and stared blankly out the window.

A rider was crossing the grass. She leapt to her feet and pressed her hands to the panes. She could only see the top of his dark head as he pulled off his hat in preparation to enter the house. Could it be Hunter?

Her heart began pounding heavily in her ears. There was a brisk knock on the door. She flew to her chair and began stitching wildly.

"Lord Thomas Westhaven to see you, milady," the butler intoned, just as she realized that Hunter was very unlikely to knock on the door of his own house.

"Thomas," she held out her hands as she rose to greet him, smiling through her disappointment.

"I thought I would come and see how you are getting on," he said brightly as he picked an invisible piece of lint off the arm of his jacket.

"I am fine. You just missed Hunter, though. He just left not two hours ago. He has business to attend to in London. It is very unfortunate, and he wanted me to go with him, but I thought I would be more comfortable here. He will be back soon."

"We were honored with a visit from my brother this morning on his way out of the park." Thomas examined his fingernails closely.

Amelia rang for tea before she responded. "I was hoping that he would visit your mother before he left. How is she?"

"Very well." He rose from his seat and began to roam the room.

"Is something the matter?"

"No." Thomas examined the abandoned embroidery frame which was decorated freely with untidy knots of floss. "Very pretty," he said vaguely.

She watched him in silence and waited for him to come to the point.

At last he turned to her and grinned sheepishly. "Dash it all, Millie, I just wanted to make sure that you were all right."

"I am." She gave him a wan smile.

"Why did he go?"

"I don't know."

Thomas' scowl was very much like his brother's. "Were you quarreling? Forgive my impertinence, Millie. I should not ask."

"I suppose we were." She waited until the maid had set down the tea tray and exited the room before she continued. "I do not understand him, Thomas."

"Nor do I."

"I don't believe he ever loved me." She was surprised to hear how matter-of-fact her voice sounded. Hearing the words aloud made her throat hurt.

"Nonsense," he replied bracingly.

"No, I am quite right." She poured him a cup of tea, willing her hand to remain steady. "He told me he only married me because he felt sorry for me."

Thomas started forward. "Impossible!"

"Quite true I am afraid. He was hoping he would get killed in Spain in order to be released from his obligation.

"He could not have meant it."

"Well, at times he seems to be quite comfortable and happy with me, and then it all falls apart for some reason I cannot fathom." She shrugged lightly, as though it did not matter.

He set down his cup and began to pace the room again. Amelia was forcibly reminded of Hunter. "Do not take it personally, Millie. Everyone finds him changed. He left Mama in tears when he shouted at her not to cling to him. He needs to be alone and will come back when he has resolved whatever is eating him."

"I wish I could be as confident." She set her cup primly on the table and composed her hands in her lap. "It is of no importance. I have decided to pursue my own interests."

"Which are?"

She shot him a look of annoyance. "Well, I don't know just yet. Perhaps I will take up gardening."

"Well, you should give up on needlework." He was re-examining the mauled embroidery piece.

Amelia could not help but laugh. "I have loved Hunter since I was a child. He could never fulfill my expectations. It was only infatuation. Perhaps I never really loved him at all." She sighed heavily. "Apparently it is vulgar to base a marriage on love anyway. We shall keep separate residence."

"I think you should go after him." Thomas turned on her with an expression of decision.

"No!" She regarded him with horror. "You do not understand. My unconditional love repulses him."

Thomas scowled out the window for a moment. "Perhaps you are right. I don't mean that you should give up on him"—he turned quickly and regarded her steadily—"but perhaps you should wait and see how things go. I care about both of you, and I want to see Hunter happy. He is dying slowly here. England is killing him as surely as Spain. He needs a purpose. He was trained to lead and there is nothing for him here but leisure."

He sat down on the couch and took Amelia's hand in his own. "Don't give up on him just yet. He needs you. He doesn't know it, but he does."

"Merciful heavens, Thomas, I am beginning to think that you have an excess of romanticism. Is it possible that you would have received a double dose while Hunter got none?" She laughed. "You worry far too much about us, and I have contributed to your worry by telling you all kinds of maudlin things. Forgive me. We will let Hunter chase his ghosts, and we will have a lovely time while you are here. I do hope that you will continue on here and not hie back to London just yet. I shall have my family over for a dinner party. You should see Miriam—she is as big as a barn. Just think of all the fun we shall have taunting her."

"I don't really see how that will be amusing," Thomas said doubtfully. "But I will stay on for a while—to make sure that you are all right."

"Don't be foolish. I have a good mind to punish you by inviting all your London belles up to Crownhaven for a long country visit."

Thomas laughed and stood up. "I see I am beaten. You do not wish to talk, and I will not pry." He bowed over her hand. "Don't give up on him, Millie. He needs you to love him," he said seriously, his dark eyes startlingly reminiscent of his brother's.

Amelia clenched her teeth and swallowed hard. It did not seem to matter whether she continued to love Hunter or not. He would not be there to see it.

Twelve

"Well, Carter." Amelia pushed back the chair at the large mahogany desk and closed the ledger. "That settles the accounts for this week. I am pleased to hear that the improvements are going so well. It is fortunate that it has not been so wet the last few weeks. I was beginning to think that we would have to wait until next spring to build the second storehouse."

"Indeed, ma'am. We have been lucky with the weather at last, and it looks as though the wheat crop may be all right after all. His lordship ordered extra stores to be delivered, which I think may stand us in good stead, since the crop isn't likely to be enough, even with the good weather."

Amelia nodded and tried to look as though she already knew this information. It was difficult to keep from feeling jealous that Hunter wrote Carter more than herself. "Do we need to hire more people for the harvest?"

Carter laughed his dry laugh. "No, ma'am, though it is like you to think ahead on that. I doubt we shall have so much to take in that we shall not be able to manage it ourselves. It is a poor crop indeed this year, but it will be precious enough, even with the extra stores." He set down his teacup, the porcelain looking ludicrously fragile in his big hands. "I hope the weather holds." His stoic face creased slightly as he rose and paced to the window. "I don't like to worry you, but there is a storm in the air."

"How soon can we finish harvesting?"

"None but the highest-lying fields were ready until now. The rest of the lands need at least another week, but I daresay we don't have that long. We will start with the south field tomorrow." He held back the heavy drapes of Hunter's study and eyed the sky with an expression of foreboding.

Amelia scowled. Running the estate was nothing like running the household. There were so many frustrating variables. She absently rubbed the quill underneath her chin. Hunter would say that she had no right to thrust herself into the management of Crownhaven, and that he and Carter had no need of her meddling. She threw down the pen and stood up. Well, if Hunter were here to take care of things instead of hiding from her in Town, there would be no need for her to meddle.

"I will come out to oversee things tomorrow."

"There is no need of that your ladyship," Carter replied firmly.

"No, I didn't mean that you were not perfectly capable of handling things yourself. I only mean that I might be able to help."

Carter apparently tried not to look scornful, but he did not entirely succeed. "Forgive my saying so, ma'am, but I don't see how you would be useful. You do very well in the managing of things, but don't you be getting overzealous and try to do everything."

"I am only following through on Lord Westhaven's plans," Amelia replied, wondering if the estate manager guessed at the rift between her and her husband. She shot a glance at him, but he had gone back to examining the horizon. She herself could only guess at what Hunter wanted for Crownhaven, while Carter had spe-

cific direction from him from London. It was ludicrous
when she thought about it. She parted with the big man,
assuring him that she would stay out of his way, and
went downstairs to find Mrs. Egan.

Amelia woke early the next morning, aware that
something was wrong. There was a strange feeling in
the air that could only mean that Carter had been right.
She rose and went to the window. The sun had barely
lugged itself over the horizon and sat sulking and white
in the overcast sky. She pulled on her dressing gown
and slipped into the rooms across the hall to evaluate
the western sky. It did not bode well. The low, dark
masses of clouds did not look like those that held a
brief summer cloudburst.

She returned to her room and struggled into a dress.
Surely the servants knew if the tenants planned to take
in the grain today. She hurried down the stairs, stuffing
her hair under a cap as she descended.

"What is happening?" she demanded breathlessly
when she reached the kitchen door.

"What do you mean, milady?" Cook sleepily looked
up from her mixing bowl.

"The crops, the rain, what will they do?"

"I am sure I don't know. It is very early for you to be
worrying about such things. Carter can manage, I am
sure. That is what you pay him for, isn't it?" She liber-
ated several eggs from their shells with rapid whacks.
The ensuing beating seemed to absorb Cook's entire
attention, so after a few moments of thought, Amelia
whisked up the stairs to Hunter's study. She penned a
quick note to Carter, hunted up a bleary-eyed footman,
and then sat down to watch the clouds and wait.

She had already changed into her riding habit preparatory to riding out to the fields when his reply arrived several hours later.

"He just said that they was up to their necks in work and for you not to be uneasy," the footman repeated doggedly in response to her anxious questioning.

Amelia paced the room several times and then went again to the window. "Have all the footmen and grooms go down and help Carter," she said decisively, turning to meet the wary eyes of the messenger.

"Ma'am?" he looked dumbfounded.

"I want everyone to go and help Carter. The storm will break by the end of the afternoon, and there is far too much work to be done."

"But, milady, that is the tenant's work," he objected.

Amelia stared at him. "Hillard, I know your parents are drygoods people in Little Hissings, and perhaps you think that the crop doesn't have anything to do with you, but I assure you that it does. If the crop is not gathered in, the tenants will have nothing to sell; they will have no money to spend in your family's store. Lord Westhaven will be forced to buy food for the tenants to keep them from starving and he might not have enough to even pay your salary." This last was a complete falsehood, but it served its purpose. The footman blinked in surprise and then sped off to deliver her order.

She had cause to regret the hastiness of her decision when she went to the stables several minutes later to find that there was no one there to saddle her horse. As she fumbled with the buckles and straps herself, Sarah appeared like an anxious ghost at her elbow.

"What is happening, your ladyship?" she whispered urgently, hopping from one foot to the other.

"Don't be frightened." Amelia muttered an unladylike curse and rubbed her pinched finger. "I have sent the men down to help gather in the tenant's crops, and

I am going myself to check on things. There is no need to panic."

"Could I go, too, ma'am?" She was still whispering, though there was no one around.

"Why would you want to?"

"My brother farms here. I could help him. Could I please go?"

"Very well. I daresay we shall both be asked to leave anyway. Can you ride?" She pulled on a stirrup to assess the stability of her handiwork.

"No, ma'am."

"Well I suppose you can ride behind me if you are not frightened."

"No, ma'am." Sarah quivered, eyeing the beast with wide eyes.

Amelia tightened the girth another notch, mounted at the block and managed, with a great deal of struggling, to haul Sarah up behind her. Their progress was impeded by the maid's intermittent shrieks of terror, but Amelia pressed the mare on, always mindful of the dark clouds rolling in.

By the time they reached the southern edge of the fields the wind had picked up. Amelia could see the workers spread out in a line, each bent nearly double as they swept the stalks of wheat down with their sickles. Jamming her riding hat tighter onto her head, she rode over to where she could see Carter directing a group of women who were gathering and tying the loose wheat into bushels.

"What are you doing here, your ladyship? I told you to stay away." He scowled as he wiped his sweating brow with a dirty kerchief.

Amelia ignored him. "Shall I ride into town and hire more men?" she asked calmly.

Carter laughed in his peculiar, grim manner. "Forgive me, your ladyship. I've already done it. I knew you would allow it, seeing as we are in a desperate situation. I thank you for sending your house men down. It has made a mighty difference." He began loading the sheaves of wheat into a wagon. "We've finished four ricks so far just today. We just might get the most of it in." He squinted at the sky. "It will be a close race though. A close race indeed."

Amelia slid off her mount, and Sarah less gracefully followed suit. "We will help," she announced.

"Now, ma'am. There is no need for you to be a martyr. You have done plenty."

"I could help," her maid piped. "I was a tier for three summers on the land my brother farms."

"Then Sarah will show me how," Amelia said, with more resolution than she felt. She tied the mare to an old hurdle that had been used to pen in sheep during the spring, when those animals inhabited a different part of the wheat field each night in order to provide fertilizer for the crops. The mare showed her breeding by contemptuously turning her back on the laborers and foraging eagerly for fallen heads of wheat. Carter shrugged and continued loading the wagon.

Sarah fell in with the line of women who were tying the bundles of wheat into sheaves. Amelia watched her carefully and then dropped to her knees and tried it herself.

Any secret superiority she had felt over her maid for the girl's lack of horsemanship was quickly forgotten. Whereas Sarah's bushel had obediently curled into a graceful sheaf with its pretty waist belted with a cord of twisted stalks, Amelia's end result was more of a mess than the original pile left by the gatherers. Somehow her bushel refused to be marshaled into bundles resembling anything but haystacks topped with a snaky coil of slowly untwisting binding stalks.

When the worker behind her went to throw the

bushel into the wagon, it instantly disintegrated into a flying whirl of chaff and dust. Amelia saw him make a face at his companion, obviously imparting the sentiment: first the weather and now this.

It got better and it got worse. Soon she was able to tie a passable bushel and could almost keep up with the slowest of the tiers. Oh, but it was miserable. The sky was growing darker by the minute, and the wind blew dirt and particles of chaff into her eyes and clothes. Her knees ached from kneeling over the bushels, and her back felt permanently hunched. Her trim Limerick riding gloves soon proved entirely unsuitable for the work of a tier, so she stripped them off and tucked them into her belt. Her habit was filthy and full of itchy bits of wheat. She stopped only to look at the sky.

"Oh, your ladyship. You really should not be working so hard. You look as though you will drop from the heat." Sarah pulled her up by the elbow and pressed a wet handkerchief to her forehead.

"Nonsense. I am fine. I only feel foolish that I am so slow." She took a deep drink of water from the dipper Sarah held out to her. There was a remarkable amount of chaff floating on top of the water in the bucket. "I am sure I am quite red-faced," she gasped. "How do you manage to go on so well?"

"Oh, ma'am, it's terribly hard work. But we all know it will be over soon. And then we will have the Harvest Home celebration. You will let me go to that, won't you, ma'am?"

Amelia could think of nothing nicer than a hot bath and a cool bed, but she nodded. How was Sarah so tireless? She rubbed her chafed hands together and noted regretfully that she was scratched in a million places. She had bent back over her bushel of wheat when she heard a shout. Several of the workers were waving their hats at a rider coming over the hill.

"It's Lord Westhaven!" the woman tying next to her exclaimed. "All the way back from London!"

Amelia felt her heart drop into her stomach and begin to pound furiously. Resisting the urge to drop back to her knees and work on as though she had not seen him, she stood straight and watched him approach.

"Carter, my God! You have gotten everyone out to work for you today," he shouted, dismounting from his horse. "I never thought I should see Allan out here, working like a fieldhand." He indicated his head groom, and laughed heartily. His laughter died away when his eyes fastened on her.

"And my wife, too. You outdo yourself, Carter."

"She insisted on helping, your lordship," the estate manager replied with a helpless gesture.

"Well then, I can hardly be remiss in my own duties," he said dryly. "We must hurry. I outran the rain, but I would say you only have an hour or two left."

Carter squinted toward the southwest and nodded. "It will be close."

Hunter removed his coat and wordlessly relieved a tenant of his sickle. He did not cast her a second glance.

She was aware of him. She felt his presence even though he was yards and yards away, working with an intensity that made her hope that he was paying more attention to the sharp blade of his sickle than she was to her tying. She herself could no longer concentrate. Somehow her sheaves reverted to their former habit of escaping from their bonds and slipping untidily to the ground. The sky grew darker.

She could hear the murmur of the workers grow louder as the tension grew. As Carter had said, it would be close. Slow, fat raindrops were beginning to fall lazily from the heavy clouds as the men reached the end of the field. At shouted orders from Carter, who was enveloped in a cloud of swirling chaff at the end of the wagon he was loading, the men dropped their sickles and began to help the women with the last of the gathering and tying.

"What are you doing out here?" Hunter demanded quietly at her elbow.

"I thought I could help," she panted, wrestling with her sheaf.

"Who ordered the men from the house out here?"

"I did." She could not look at him. "I knew you would have done so." *If you had been here,* she added silently.

He did not reply, but bent to tie a sheaf. Amelia suppressed the faint sense of satisfaction she felt at seeing the wheat sliding from his unwieldy bundle. They moved on, working together, silent and determined.

"It's coming down too fast. We'll take what we have and take it down to where the ricks are." Carter wiped the raindrops from his face and called the other workers in. Collecting their sickles, he handed them into the last wagon which was only half full of wheat.

"We didn't lose much." Amelia collapsed to the bottom of the wagon as it lurched forward. She squinted over the raggedy field. It was hard to believe how much ground they had covered. Several small, lower lying fields remained unshorn, but the wheat was still green there and would have to be counted a loss. She rubbed her aching neck.

"Did you work all day?" Hunter moved her hands gently and took over the task. The feel of his hands made her shoulders more tense. She frowned as her body betrayed her with an excruciating wash of desire.

"Hardly," she laughed scornfully. "Half as long as everyone else. They must have been up at dawn." His hands against her skin were making her whole body go shaky. She was glad she was sitting down.

"I could not believe it when I saw you there. You looked so beautiful—so natural."

She turned her head to look at him over her shoulder. "Natural? You mean filthy. There is not a single part of me that does not itch. I shudder to think of the insects that have been living in the field." Her laugh sounded strange to her own ears.

"I should have come back sooner." His voice was so close to her cheek she could feel his breath as he exhaled a sigh. "Carter told me you were managing things so well, I decided I was hardly needed."

Amelia turned on him. "Yes," she said urgently, "you are needed very much." An unreadable expression of perplexity and tenderness crossed his face. She was painfully aware that they were not alone in the jolting, dirty wagon. She wanted very much to throw herself against his chest in a very unladylike way. Thunder sounded in the distant southwest and the rain responded with a more determined sprinkling.

"Carter! Carter! Your lordship!" A man came running full tilt up the dirt track. "You must come at once! The wagon—there's been an accident!"

Thirteen

The tenants and workers responded to the news of the accident with a frenzy of undirected activity. Hunter and Carter, along with several other of the workers leapt from the cart and ran down the road toward the ricks. The driver of the cart whipped the horse to a bone-jarring trot that flung the remaining occupants of the wagon on top of one another.

When they arrived at the scene a moment later, a large group of people was gathered around the second wagon.

"Get back to work! We'll take care of things here!" Carter was shouting ineffectually. "We have to get the ricks up on the staddles before the ground gets too wet. Someone run for the tarps, you fools!" He tried to push away the group that jostled to see what was happening. "We'll take care of things here!"

Amelia pushed through the crowd, not caring who she elbowed out of the way. She could see Hunter crouched on the ground beside a prostrate form.

The young man was dead when she arrived. In his haste to jump from the wagon, he had slipped beneath its heavy wheel. She gasped and felt her stomach lurch as she looked at his still body. Like everyone else at the front of the crowd, she felt paralyzed—unaware of the shoving she was receiving from behind from other on-lookers anxious to find out what had happened.

"Everyone, get back to work. Finish the ricks. *Now.*" Hunter's voice jarred the tenants back to life, and they obeyed without question. He pulled the young man's body from beneath the wagon's wheel and ordered the driver to move on. The man looked to be about nineteen or twenty years old at most. A boy really. His pale hair fell back from his dirty forehead, and the rain splashed insolently onto his strangely expressionless face. It was one of the Hart boys. She remembered seeing him at his parents' house when she visited them during the illness of their youngest child. Amelia heard Hunter shouting for someone to fetch the man's family as she staggered behind a rick to vomit quietly.

She was not sure how long she stayed there, on her hands and knees in the rain, weeping, when Sarah found her.

"Oh, your ladyship, I was so worried about you. It's so terrible." She stooped down and peered into her mistress's face. "Cast up your accounts, did you? Well, I can't say that I blame you. I felt a little pukey myself." She pulled Amelia to her feet and smoothed her hair from her face. "You can come out now. They've moved him to his mother's house. Powerful upset she was, as you can imagine."

"Oh, Sarah, what a terrible thing to have happened," she moaned.

"Terrible indeed. But I suppose we should be glad it happened once we were nearly done and not in the middle of the day. But it was a terrible thing indeed."

Amelia looked at Sarah in wonder. The girl was upset, but she took the accident as almost a matter of course. How could she handle these things so stoically? She felt a fresh wave of nausea at the memory of the incident. "Where is Hunter?"

"He's with the family. Don't you worry about him. Look, ma'am, someone has brought your horse down. Let's go back to the house. There is nothing more you can do here."

Amelia allowed herself to be led, like her mare, back to the house. It was a long walk, but she did not feel up to riding, and Sarah did not raise any objections to abstaining from another pillion ride. By the time they had reached the house, the rain had shaken off its lethargy and was roaring down with a purpose. Amelia felt so tired she could barely lift one foot in front of the other. It hardly seemed to matter that she was soaked to the skin. She had probably been so for hours.

She silently handed the animal over to a groom who looked as tired as she felt herself. The mare alone had the energy to dance about in protest against the lightning-filled sky.

"I'll have a bath brought up to you, your ladyship," Sarah offered as she practically supported Amelia up the stairs.

"Thank you. Ask someone who was not in the fields today to do it. I am sure everyone must be more tired than me." She collapsed on the seat at her dressing table, glad for a chance to think alone for a moment. Everything had happened all at once. For weeks she had done nothing but make the infinitely unimportant decisions that they would have lamb for dinner on Wednesday and goose on Thursday, and now, suddenly, the world had fallen in on her.

She stared in surprise at her reflection in the glass. Her habit, which had once been dark blue was a brownish gray. There were bits of chaff in her hair and dark smears of dirt across her face where she had wiped her sweating brow. A rip at the neck of the habit showed the white skin beneath and contrasted starkly with the dark ring of dust around her neckline.

Oh, she had felt like such a heroine today. Carter had been right. She had been playing the martyr and thinking that she could single-handedly save the crops by going out and working beneath her station. How humbled she felt. She had been useless at the work and now . . . now this boy had been killed, and she was helpless. How vain she had been to think that she could control things.

Mrs. Egan herself escorted two girls up with the bath water and fussed affectionately as she helped her into the tub.

"Milady, I could not believe my ears when I heard that you were out in the fields. You working like a hired hand—it is a shame. That's what it is, a shame. Everyone belowstairs says that you are a great lady, going out like that to save the crop, but I think it is a shame when the lady of the house has to go into the fields. Haven't we got enough here? Is his lordship so poor that he cannot hire help? Is he so poor that his wife must work in the fields?"

"Hunter was working, too," Amelia said tiredly.

"Oh, I know. It just breaks my heart to see you so dirty and tired. You are likely to kill yourself with working so hard. And look at your hands—ruined! I will have one of the girls bring up a salve."

"Thank you. I will be fine. I don't think I need anything else," she said with finality. Mrs. Egan left at last, still clucking about the shame of it all. At last she was alone again, steeping in the warm water and wondering what she would do about Hunter.

The whole world was tumbling and then he had to arrive. And then the accident on top of that. Dragging herself out of the bath at last, she tried to remind herself that he was so much more capable of handling the tragedy than she was. If he had not come, she would be the one comforting that young man's family. She would be expected to know the etiquette of the situation. It was really a blessing that he had come, she assured herself. But it didn't feel like a blessing. She could only remember the feel of his hands on her shoulders, and the agonizing realization that just when she thought she had shaken off the love she felt for him, it had jumped out to strangle her.

She was sitting at her dressing table, tiredly picking at a cold collation, when there was a knock at the door. It was a genuine knock, not a servant's scratch. She felt her stomach constrict.

"Come in," she managed, after a hard swallow.

Hunter entered, brows drawn. "Things are pretty well settled, I suppose," he said with a sigh. He wiped his dirty forehead with his dirty hand. His once-immaculate linen was now a sweat-stained brown.

"His family?" She pulled the edges of her wrapper closer around her throat. Without his coat, he was somehow almost distressingly masculine.

"They are distraught, of course. I did what I could. We will have the funeral Saturday."

"Oh, Hunter. I feel so terrible. What an awful thing to have happened. I am sorry I ran away. I just . . . I just couldn't . . ." Her throat constricted at the memory.

"There was nothing to be done. Carter managed the crew putting the tarps over the ricks. You did enough." He leaned his back against the closed door and looked at her intently.

Uncomfortable under his gaze, she turned back to her meal. "Have you eaten?"

"I will get something later. I must wash up now. I just wanted to let you know that everything was taken care of." His attention seemed suddenly absorbed by a piece of bedraggled linen that had come loose from his cuff.

"Thank you. I am so glad you were here to manage things. If this had happened while you were away . . ."

"You would have been fine." He paused, frowning at his cuff. Amelia desperately cast about in her mind for something to say. At last he continued with a gruff laugh. "I don't know what to say to you. I could not believe my eyes when I saw you there working in the field. You have managed the estate as though you were born to do it." He pulled off the entire strip of fabric with a savage jerk.

"Nonsense, you were the one managing it."

"That is untrue. Carter told me in every letter of your excellent business sense." He tied the linen into a knot and pulled it tight.

She realized that she had unconsciously reached out her hands to him, and she returned them to her lap. "I was only trying to help. I was only trying to do what you would do."

His hands dropped to his sides. "You are a remarkable woman. Thank you for today." He looked at her, his dark eyes agonizingly sad. "You made me very proud."

Amelia drew a breath that caught on a sob in her throat. She opened her mouth again to beg him to come to her, dirt and all, but he had bowed and left the room.

She awoke with a start from a troubled sleep and lay tense and confused for a moment. What had woken her? She heard the noise again, the muffled sound of an intense conversation. She pulled on her dressing gown and stepped silently over to the door that connected her room with Hunter's. He was having one of his nightmares. She remembered them from when they first married, but Hunter would allow only Caldwell, his valet and former batman, to wake him. But Hunter had ridden to Crownhaven alone, and Caldwell was still in London. She tentatively entered the room and stood by the bed as he hoarsely carried on a disjointed monologue, twisting the bed linens with his restless turnings. Without pausing to think, she climbed into the bed beside him.

"Hunter!" She gave him a firm shake.

He sat upright with a gasp like a drowning man erupting to the surface. "What!" he bellowed, then looked about him in confusion.

Amelia gently forced him to lie down beside her. "You were only dreaming."

He looked at her, blinking as though he did not recognize her. She smoothed his hair back from his damp forehead.

"That boy . . ." His voice was ragged.

"I know. But there was nothing you could do." She continued to caress his brow, unsure of how to soothe him.

"I killed him."

"Hunter, it was an accident. There was nothing anyone could have done."

His breathing was heavy and labored. He didn't seem fully awake. "I was in charge of everyone. I should have been more careful."

"There is no way you could have foreseen it happening." She lay down and fit her body to his. He did not move away.

He grabbed his temples with one hand and rubbed them slowly. "It was just like Ciudad-Rodrigo. There was nothing I could do." His voice grew low. "I am a bad leader, Millie."

She threw an arm violently around his neck. "I will not have you say that. You were mentioned in so many dispatches. You were a marvelous leader. You were a hero."

"How I hate that word." He rolled over to face her, his eyes shining strangely in the half light. "I could not save them. They trusted me, and I could not save them."

"Your job was not to save them. It was to lead them. People do not go fight wars without knowing that there are risks. No one blames you for preventing what you had no control over."

"And then today . . ."

"Today is the same. If you had not come home today, the accident might have happened just the same." She tightened her arm about his neck. "Do you understand me?" she asked sternly.

He rolled back onto his back and did not reply, but stared blindly into the darkness. It was so strange to be comforting him. He felt so warm beside her through the muslin of her nightrail. It was so intensely intimate to be pressed against the length of his body. She dreaded the ultimate moment when he would pull away from her and shut her out from his psyche.

He closed his eyes and breathed slowly for a moment. "It will take a long time," he said in a low voice, just when she began to think that he had fallen back to sleep.

"Yes," she whispered, "it will."

She felt his hand warm on her shoulder. It slid down her arm to her hand and pressed it.

The sun was stabbing in through a gap in the curtains when she woke. At first she was disoriented by the strangeness of the bed and the weight across her stomach. She tried to disentangle herself, but Hunter pulled her closer and curled his body around hers. She laced her fingers with his. It must be very late in the morning.

They had stayed awake talking. Hunter must have talked for hours about Spain and the troops there, his voice tense with pride when he described the men he had commanded there.

And then, then when he had talked himself silent at last, he had made love to her. It was not like the carnal passion of their lovemaking in the cottage during the storm, and it was not like those many impersonal couplings since their marriage. This time it was intense, personal—she knew that it was her, her alone, that he was focused on. The memory of it made her pulse quicken.

She knew she would be unable to sleep any longer, so she slid from the bed and went to her own room to dress. That trip alone made her entire body protest. Her back ached from stooping in the field over the bushels of grain and there was not a muscle in her arms that did not have its own specific complaint. Sarah must have come up with her chocolate, for it sat cooling by the empty bed. At least the girl had the good sense not to rouse the house over her disappearance. She was beaming smugly when she answered Amelia's summons.

"Oh, Sarah, I can barely move today," Amelia moaned as she struggled into a day dress.

"You should stay abed. The crops are in; there is no reason for you to be about." The maid sat her down and began dressing her hair. "But I do want to say, ma'am, everyone seems to be wondering what we will be doing about the Harvest Home festival, what with Charles Hart killed and all."

Amelia tried not to cringe. "I don't know. I will ask Lord Westhaven. The funeral will be tomorrow. I would not wish his family to feel as though we are being disrespectful, but I also would not wish to disappoint the tenants. They certainly worked beyond the call of duty yesterday." She mused over the situation while Sarah finished her hair.

Hunter did not appear at breakfast, so she went about her normal household duties. He must have slipped out of the house while she was discussing the menu with Cook, for he had obviously been out when he sat down to luncheon.

"I have been to see the Hart family," he announced.

"How are they?"

"Well enough, considering. The basket you sent arrived while I was there. That was very kind of you, Amelia."

"I would have gone myself, but I did not wish to intrude on them." She pushed the partridge around on the plate. "And I was afraid," she added.

"It was very kind," he repeated. He scowled and applied himself to the food on his plate, eating as though he did not know or care what he put in his mouth. "We will hold the Harvest Home in a fortnight. Carter and I talked it over. He will take care of everything while I am gone."

He said the last words so quietly that Amelia thought she must have misheard him.

"What? Where are you going?"

"Back to Town." He kept his eyes on his plate, sawing viciously at the meat.

Amelia's fork clattered to the plate. "Why?" she managed at last.

"Business." The word was said in a tone that brooked no discussion.

She clenched the arms of her chair until they creaked in protest. They were back where they started. Did last night mean nothing? "It was not your fault, Hunter," she insisted, feeling anger flush over her. "Do you have to take responsibility for the world? Do you think that everything happens because of you? The bad harvest, the war, death and pestilence, do they all occur because of your faults? You are very vain indeed if you think that you can change everything. Some things just happen."

"I said it was business!" he shouted, throwing down his napkin and storming out of the room.

She did not see him again until the funeral. They met in the churchyard and stood side by side during the service, and never once did their eyes meet. Amelia clenched her teeth as they received the thanks of the tenants. Everyone seemed to feel such heartfelt gratitude at their involvement with estate affairs. "See?" she felt like shouting to Hunter, "They adore you! You have done everything that is right by them!"

But he stood stiff and still by her side, making gracious replies to praise he evidently could not hear. He bowed her into the closed carriage without a word and mounted his roan.

"I shall take leave of you now, Amelia, for I am leaving shortly. Thank you for everything." His eyes met hers for the first time that day. They had the exhausted look of a hunted man. "You are a courageous woman, and I thank you, but you must let me go."

He wheeled the horse before she could formulate a reply and rode off across the fields. She watched him go, livid, but frightened. She had thought that his return was a reprieve, but he was still fighting himself. He could not return until he had won, but who could vanquish a foe like that? Oh, but she did not feel very courageous at all.

Fourteen

December 4, 1812
Charles Street

Dear Amelia,
    I hope that this letter finds you well, and I hope that
Miriam and her baby are also in good health. I have
written Lord Wells with my congratulations. I had hoped
that my business here would go more quickly, but I am
afraid that I will be somewhat longer still. I hope you
are comfortable. I am in weekly contact with Carter, so
I know that things at the estate have progressed very well
indeed. I will remain respectfully your servant,

                                H. Westhaven

Amelia smiled bitterly as she put the letter in the fire.
Business would be longer still. He had been away over
three months already, and he must know that she was
aware that there was no "business" to see to in London.
She pressed her hand to her forehead, willing her
flushed cheeks to cool. He was in weekly contact with
Carter. He wrote her three stilted lines a month. Respectfully your servant indeed! She stabbed the embers
of the letter deeper into the coals.

Slowly, she lowered herself into a chair by the fire.

The longer she waited, the worse it would get. Yes, any
longer and her family or his would unwittingly inform
him of her condition, and even though the thought of
him made her teeth ache with the clenching, she could
not intentionally humiliate him. She drew several deep
breaths and stared at the fire.

The wet summer had quickly given way to a wet fall
soon after Hunter had left. Many of his projects, the
drainage, the re-roofing of the tenants' cottages had
been postponed. The tenants were anxious about the
coming winter, as their crops had been poor. But
Hunter knew all of these things. Where before he had
been intent upon managing every aspect of the estate
down to the most trivial detail, now he was content to
leave everything in Carter's hands. They were capable
enough. Carter had bought more grain at astronomical
prices to ensure that no one would go hungry. He had
managed to make many of the renovations despite the
weather. But it was worrying that Hunter no longer
cared to be a part of these decisions.

Amelia forced herself to get up from the chair and
go to the desk. She drew her shawl closer around her
as she seated herself in front of the sheet of paper. It
was cold in this part of the room. She should have asked
Evans to make up the fire a little bigger. If Hunter only
wrote her more, she would have quite a large blaze, she
thought with a bitter laugh. She cut her quill and then
focused herself to compose the letter she had tried to
write every day since he had left.

December 6, 1812
Crownhaven

Dear Hunter,
  *I hope that this letter finds you well. I know I should
have written you sooner, but I had hoped that you would*

*come home, so that I could give you this news myself. If
all goes well you shall have an heir in May. Do not be
anxious about me, as everything*

She broke off and read what she had written. *As
everything is fine? Hardly.* She slowly crumpled the
sheet of paper into a tight ball. It didn't matter if
Hunter didn't write her. She generated quite enough
paper to burn on her own. As she crossed to the
hearth, she caught a glimpse of herself in the mirror
on the mantel. She caught her breath. Her eyes had
dark smudges under them and her complexion was
pale and dull. She hadn't remembered what dress she
had put on this morning.

She thought again about the night she had shaken
him from his nightmare. That must have been the night
she conceived. Perhaps she should have felt bitter, considering his defection the next day, but the memory
somehow remained comfortable and warm.

Below the mirror on the mantelpiece lay a small pile
of debris. She touched it gently, but another piece of
it disintegrated into dust beneath her fingertips. It was
the wreath of wildflowers that Hunter had made for her
that summer day. She picked it up and made a sweeping
gesture to throw it into the fire after her letter, but she
stopped herself. She stood holding the dry, bedraggled
crown for a long moment and then at last placed it back
where it had lain.

She rang the bell for Wedgeworth. This was outside
of enough.

"Wedgeworth, please ask Sarah to have my things
packed. I am going to London tomorrow. Also, could
you have the carriage brought round in half an hour?
I will visit the Dower House before I leave."

She had seen her own family only two days before,
so she wrote a carefully worded note informing them

of her departure and implying that Hunter had asked
for her to come to London. That would please her
mother. She had been prying for months, trying to dis-
cover what could possibly be keeping Hunter away.
Amelia had invented some extremely elaborate excuses.
She must remember to inform Hunter that he was on
the board of trustees of a London foundling's hospital
and a reviewer of acquisitions at the National Gallery.

"Lady Westhaven." The dowager entered the drawing room with a perplexed expression. "I did not expect
you until Wednesday. Is anything the matter?"

"No. Everything is fine." Amelia forced herself to
smile.

"Have you had news from Hunter? I got a letter from
him just three days ago. I must say, it strikes me as extremely peculiar that he should wish to spend so much
time away from you. I declare, he has been away longer
than he was here!" The lines between the dowager's
nose and mouth deepened. "I am beginning to suspect
that you drove him away." She gave a tittering little
laugh to show that she was only teasing. When she was
finished, she frowned again. "I will live out my days
shuffled away in this damp little house, but I at least
expected to have the assurance of the continuation of
the Westhaven line and the presence of my son to comfort me." She rang for tea and seated herself with a
slight regal motion that Amelia should do the same.

Amelia sat down and prepared herself for the usual
litany.

"Now, it seems as though I shall be deprived of that,
my only comfort in a bleak, harsh existence. I have always loved you like a daughter, Lady Westhaven. It pains
me to think that I could have nursed a viper to my
bosom. What is it that makes Hunter's ancestral home

so unpleasant to him? So unpleasant that he cannot bear to write his mother above once a month, not to mention come home."

"I am going to join Hunter in London, ma'am," Amelia interrupted. She felt a wisp of pleasure at the dowager's stunned silence.

"He has asked you to come at last, eh? Well, you shall find Town very flat this time of year I should say. There is absolutely no one in London during fox hunting season. You'll have little enough to do until the little season begins, and I daresay that even that will be flat enough. No one of real quality would even consider going to Town before April."

"I shall leave tomorrow."

"Tomorrow? Well, I do hope that you will bring Hunter directly back. I don't know how I am expected to get on in this dismal little hovel during the worst weather of the year."

"I am sure that Hunter would be happy to set you up in Town if you wish to go." Amelia rose and gathered her wrap about her, preparatory to leaving.

"Indeed not! I would never wish to keep my son on leading strings. But you must tell him, Lady Westhaven, that we will all celebrate Christmas together. Thomas is coming back from Scotland, so Hunter must be here."

"Of course, ma'am." Amelia left, wondering why three years ago Lady Camilla Westhaven had not simply written to the general and ordered her son home from Spain.

Amelia patted her curls self-consciously and leaned forward to look out the carriage window. The town house was just at the end of the street. She had a feeling that the knot in her stomach was not due just to the sickness of early pregnancy. Allowing the footman to hand her carefully down the steps when she would much rather leap down and run to the door, she tried to calm her thoughts. Hunter would not be too angry. After all, the worst he could do would be to send her home. She squeezed her hands together; there could be nothing worse than that.

The knocker was off the door. But that didn't make sense; all his letters were addressed from here. She tilted her head back and looked up at the windows. They were unshuttered, but the drapes were drawn. She hesitated, unsure whether to pound on the door or to walk directly in. She glanced back at the coachman and footmen who were watching with interest. Well, she was mistress of the house after all. She drew a sharp breath, opened the door, and walked in.

It was dark inside. She stood for a moment with her back to the door and waited for her eyes to adjust. It was still dark.

"Hello?" she called out, feeling extremely stupid. Where was the butler? She entered a small receiving room. The curtains were drawn, and there was a thick layer of dust on all of the furniture. The dining room was the same, but with less dust. She mounted the stairs, calling out to the servants, but no one answered. The upstairs drawing rooms were much like the rest of the house. Drapes drawn, neat, though obviously uncared for. She paused with her hand on the door to Hunter's study. There were footsteps at the back of the house coming closer.

"Hello?"

"Oh, Lady Westhaven!" Mrs. Jennings, the cook, panted up the stairs, wiping her hands on her apron. "Oh, milady! Whatever are you doing here? I didn't know that you was coming into Town. Oh, I would have fixed things up if I knew you was coming." She seized her apron and began twisting it.

"What has happened?"

"Oh, your ladyship! His lordship dismissed all the servants months ago. He only kept me on so I could cook for him. He dismissed every one, even the ones who had been here for years. They was devastated, they was. To be fair, he did write letters for those who wanted positions and pensioned off the older ones, but oh, ma'am, we was all mortally surprised."

"Where is he?" She pressed down the fear that clutched her.

"Oh, Lady Westhaven, I don't know. I mostly stay in the kitchen as he likes it. I only came up because I heard you calling. He don't like me to ask where he goes."

"Will he be back tonight? Surely he must have left you instructions."

"I don't know, ma'am. He says I should cook what I want and not wait on him. Sometimes he does not come back for days."

Amelia looked at her, horrified. At last she found her voice. "Open the drapes. Open the windows, too. See if you can find someone who will help clean up the place. Have them air out my room. I will ask my outriders to help you, and I will help you myself once I have put my head on straight." She pressed her fingertips to her temples and drew a deep breath.

"Are you ill your ladyship? This must be an awful shock. Shall I call the doctor?"

"No. I am fine. Please. I cannot stand the closeness in here. Please help me open the windows."

"I'll get the men from the stables to do that. Just sit yourself down for a moment."

Amelia nodded vaguely and watched Mrs. Jennings disappear down the servant stairs. She pushed open the door to Hunter's study. Unlike the rest of the house, this room showed undeniable signs of occupancy. Dirty dishes and cravats littered the floor. There was an untidy pile of papers placidly soaking up ink from the over-turned standish. Bits of broken glass were sprayed about the fireplace where someone had evidently disposed of one of the matching crystal claret glasses. The corresponding decanter was unstopped and empty, coated with a sticky residue at the bottom where the last bit of claret had evaporated. The airless stench of the room was unbearable.

She stifled the nausea that threatened to overcome her and stepped to the window to fling it open. Gulping breaths of fresh air and trying to master the panic that welled up inside of her, she tried to imagine what could have happened. It was obvious that Hunter was not living a carefree life of excitement and glamor. She wondered vaguely if he had lost his wits entirely. Perhaps his nerves were not as strong as she had thought, and he had lost all rational faculties. She sat down in the desk chair and looked over his correspondences, trying to find a clue to his mental state.

Underneath a plate of stale bread and a piece of cheese so desiccated it was almost unrecognizable, she found a large pile of receipts. She examined them closely, suddenly afraid that he had gambled away their entire fortune. But they were mostly purchases of grain and other foodstuff made to supplement the supply at Crownhaven. Nothing seemed unwarranted or extravagant.

She put the receipts down and continued to search, suppressing her feeling of guilt. Surely this was an emergency. Hunter had been living like an animal for three months with no rational explanation to anyone. Surely that excused looking through his effects. Another pile of papers appeared to be ordinary business correspondences, letters from his banker and lawyer and from

Carter. She was surprised to find her own name in virtually all of the estate manager's letters.

> ... As you requested, I have made inquiries into the state of Lady Westhaven's health and well-being. She spends most of her time seeing to the tenants or riding. While her health is good, her maid says that she is quiet and appears depressed in spirits. She refuses to see a doctor ...
>
> Lady Westhaven has seen to the Hargrave family's illness and attended Mrs. Ellis during her confinement. She was grief-stricken when the Ellis child was stillborn. ...
>
> Lady Westhaven has continued in her visits to the Hart family ...

So she was being spied upon! She felt a flush of anger directed at everyone at Crownhaven, but then realized that it was Hunter who she should be angry with. He was the one who had commanded everyone to report on her. She put the letters back where they had lain and sat back in the chair.

Why would Hunter have asked people to watch her? Was it because he suspected her of something? Perhaps he was worried about her. Perhaps it was because he cared.

"Ha," she said, surprised at how loud and bitter her voice sounded in the empty room. A frown gathered between her brows as she continued her searching. She didn't feel very guilty now. In the top drawer there was a jumble of paper and pens, old theatre tickets, sealing wax, one stocking, and a very maligned piece of apple tart.

In the second drawer she found letters. They were

tied up in an uncharacteristically neat bundle at the back. She took the first one from the thick stack.

> *My dearest wife,*
> *I hardly have the right to call you thus after everything that has happened between us. Every day I wake up and dress with the intention of returning to you and begging for a chance to start again. But then I recall how much I have made you suffer and how little I have deserved that love that you have constantly shown me. It was something I had as a support all my life and yet I did not realize it. Without you I am aimless, frantic, and dangerous, like the untrimmed boom of a boat.*

The letter broke off in a series of irritated scribbles. Amelia stared at it in wonder. There was no question that it was from Hunter. Was it to her? Was it possible that he had another wife? The idea made her throat close and her stomach twist painfully. She took another letter.

> *My dearest wife,*
> *I will be home in two days. I cannot express how much I long to be back at Crownhaven. I have stayed away too long. But it is not the house I have missed; it is you. How stupid I was to have left and how happy I will be to return. But I have learned during my absence that your love is the only thing that has given my life a purpose. Forgive me, Amelia. I will never let . . .*

This letter broke off, too, but Amelia pressed the existing fragment to her. It was true. He loved her. He wanted to be with her. With trembling fingers, she quickly looked through the rest of the letters. They were much the same. Each one was an aborted attempt to write her and tell her that he loved her. He had written nearly every day. Some were long and rambling, itemizing each of his wrongdoings and her angelic sufferance of his faults. Some never got past "my dearest wife." One was written in badly rhymed verse.

Amelia tied the letters up again carefully. She was unsure how to react to this sudden information. If he was so desperately in love with her, why had he left her? He would have a good deal of explaining to do when he returned.

She heard a bold knock on the door and nearly jumped out of her skin. It couldn't be him; he would just have walked in. Why would anyone come calling? The knocker was off the door. She went down the stairs, calling out to Mrs. Jennings that she would get the door herself.

"Yes?" She stared in wonder at the woman on the doorstep. She was very richly dressed in a gown of pink silk, but no woman of Quality would wear quite so much jewelry during the day. Her hat was a good deal over-trimmed, and there was some doubt that her lips were naturally such a bright cherry color. But there was no question that her fur tippet was of the highest quality, and as she stood there in the most assured manner, Amelia had no choice but to ask her her business.

"I am here to see Lord Westhaven," the woman replied, looking down her nose at Amelia as she took in her dusty traveling gown and untidy hair.

"He is not here. I am the lady of the house," Amelia said coolly, drawing herself up to her full height.

"Indeed?" The woman's expression held disdainful surprise and a sharp interest. "Oh, dear." Her face crumpled. "Oh dear, oh dear, oh dear." She swayed slightly. "But I must see his lordship." Her haughty voice gave way to a throbbing plead.

"I am afraid that I do not know when he is expected back," Amelia wavered.

"But I must! I must!" The woman's voice rose to unseemly levels and she pressed her handkerchief to her nose. She seemed to have grown quite pale and her sway increased. All at once, her knees gave way and she clutched in vain at the banister as she collapsed on the doorstep.

Fifteen

Amelia gave a squeak of surprise, stood stock-still for a moment, and then called for help. Several of the footmen who had accompanied her on her journey were presently employed helping Mrs. Jennings open the windows. They came at a run and quickly carried the prostrate stranger into the house.

Her eyelids were already beginning to flutter when they laid her on the sofa in the small receiving room off the front hallway. Mrs. Jennings was sent to fetch a vinaigrette, while Amelia applied herself to anxiously patting the woman's hands and exclaiming, "Miss! Miss!" in a distressed voice.

The woman regained consciousness with a weak moan and attempted to sit up. Amelia restrained her and murmured soothingly.

"I'm sorry. I think I fainted," the woman whispered.

"You did. I am very sorry, but I did not know you were unwell. To think, letting you faint on the doorstep! How very ungracious of me." Through her confusion, Amelia had a fleeting thought of Hunter's surprise at coming home to find not only his wife but a complete stranger who was lying with her toes cocked up on the blue and gold upholstery of the drawing room settee.

"I came to see . . . Hunter."

The woman's voice was faint, but Amelia started to

hear her clearly use her husband's Christian name.
They were interrupted at that moment by the arrival of
the vinaigrette, which Mrs. Jennings wielded so liberally
that soon all three of them had smarting eyes.

"Are you feeling better, my dear?" Mrs. Jennings
asked anxiously.

"Mrs. Jennings, would you be so good as to fetch us
some good strong tea? I will pour out a little liquor for
her." Amelia talked the cook out of the room and
poured a generous glass of brandy with shaking hands.
She turned on the woman and regarded her steadily.
"Who are you?"

"My name is Angelina La Fleur." The woman received the glass and took a tiny sip.

Angelina La Fleur. It was a rather made-up sounding
name. "And what may I do for you, Miss La Fleur?"
She tried to keep her voice kind, but she suddenly very
much wanted her guest to leave.

"I must see Hunt—I mean Lord Westhaven."

Amelia's sense of foreboding increased. "As I told
you, I do not know when he will be back. Is there anything I can help you with?"

Angelina La Fleur looked up at her with her lovely
hazel eyes filling with tears. "Oh, Lady Westhaven!" she
wailed, the slightly foreign accent slipping into pure
East London. "Oh, Lady Westhaven! What am I to do?
I—I am increasing. I am carrying Hunter's child."

Amelia's heart gave a great painful squeeze and went
bloodlessly cold. She felt her knees give way and sank
into a chair. The roaring in her ears became louder
and everything started to grow dark around the edges.
She forced herself to breathe. Only the sudden movement of her own child within her brought her back
from the brink of a faint.

"I only just discovered it myself. That is why I don't

look it." The woman smoothed her gown around her middle self-consciously.

"Indeed." It was a remarkably stupid thing to say, but then again, was there any proper response?

They stared at each other for a moment in silence. Miss La Fleur took a rather large gulp of brandy.

"Here is the tea!" Mrs. Jennings sang out as she entered the room. "I hope you are feeling better, my dear. Would you like some cake? I made some lovely tea cakes this very morning, and they were just finishing up when Lady Westhaven arrived. I will be mortally offended if you don't say you'll take some. With clotted cream? Won't that be lovely?"

"Thank you, Mrs. Jennings." Amelia was surprised to find that her voice was steady and clear, and that her traitorous hands were actually pouring out tea for the vile woman before her. She waited for the cook to leave the room.

"Does Westhaven know?" she asked at last.

"No . . . that is . . . I came to tell him today."

"Are you his mistress?" Her voice was cool and clipped.

Amelia saw a flash of triumph in those hazel eyes before the woman lowered them.

"Yes, ma'am."

Amelia unconsciously pressed her hand to her belly, as if to protect the child. She had momentary visions of both of their children growing up and playing together. She swallowed hard against the bile that rose in her throat.

"What is it that you wish for us to do?" she asked.

"Lady Westhaven, I'm desperate. I can't find another protector in this state. I have nothing! My child and I will starve in the streets!" Miss La Fleur put a trembling hand to her throat.

Amelia eyed the large rings on that trembling hand

and the fine rubies encircling the throat. "I doubt that," she said dryly. "I will speak with my husband, and we will make sure that you are provided for."

This was obviously not the response that Angelina expected. Her brows drew together. "But I must speak to Hunter! Our child!"

"I will speak to him," Amelia replied firmly. "Leave your direction, and we will contact you."

Hunter's mistress became even more confused. "But Lady Westhaven! Please do not throw me out onto the street! I beg of you!" She looked wildly about her, as though Amelia were threatening her violence.

"Please calm yourself. I assure you that you will not be thrown into the street. Shall I write down where you live?" She rose and went to the writing desk, her head feeling curiously detached from her body.

Miss La Fleur repeated her direction with a scowl. She no longer seemed hysterically confused, only irritated. "Please ask a servant to show me out." She rose and settled her skirts in a regal manner.

"I shall do it myself."

"Do you have no servants?" she demanded in surprise as Amelia led her into the hallway.

"No one at present. Were you anxious that they all know your situation?" She pinioned the woman with a level look.

Miss La Fleur made no reply other than to flounce down the front steps. Amelia examined the woman's direction with interest. It was in a rather genteel section of town. She wondered if Hunter had bought the house for her. The idea made her feel vaguely sick.

But mostly she was tired. She retired to the drawing room and sat down feeling strangely unable to react. Surely it could not be true. There was definitely something strange about Miss Angelina La Fleur. Perhaps she was only an adventuress who was hoping to extort money.

Perhaps she didn't even know Hunter at all. That would
be too good to be true. There was no point in speculat-
ing. Only her husband could answer her questions.

Hunter pulled himself up the stairs by the railing. It
was dark, but he did not bother to light himself a lamp.
He knew every step, even in the gloomy half-light. Mrs.
Jennings must have gone to bed long ago. He was glad
that he had dismissed his valet. It would be terrible to
know that he was lurking upstairs, waiting for him to
return, silently disapproving. It seemed that there was
absolutely nothing that Caldwell approved of these
days. The former batman had obviously thought that
three years of service during the Peninsular campaign
entitled him to pass judgment on his employer. He had
not taken his dismissal well.

"I'll go home to her when I bloody well like," he
growled at a silhouette cut of his great-grandmother
that was hanging at the turn of the stairs. Caldwell had
had some gall to tell him what was the right thing to
do. Though he had forced a generous settlement on the
valet, he heard that the man still hovered about the
stables.

He flung open the door of the study and blinked in
surprise. Mrs. Jenning had carelessly forgotten to bank
the fire for the night. The silly woman could have
burned the house down. It was no matter. It was not as
though he was going to sleep tonight. He stumped over
to it and began to build up the small blaze that was
burning there.

He felt Amelia's gaze before he saw her. Looking up
from his crouched position on the floor, he saw her
sitting in his big wing back chair watching him with a
blank kind of interest. In the flickering dimness that
wavered with the fire, she seemed almost other-worldly.

"What are you doing here?" he roared, leaping to his feet.

"I was waiting for you."

"Why are you here in Town?" he sputtered, vaguely relieved that she was not a phantom come to accuse him. Just the real thing come to accuse him.

"I came to see you." Her voice was as still as her face, her large eyes almost clear in the shadowy room.

"What about?" His voice softened. "Are you well? Is everything at Crownhaven all right?" He started to approach her, but hung back.

"You look very tired, Hunter." She smiled faintly. "Are you drunk?"

"No."

There was a pause. Amelia's eyes were drawn to the fire. Hunter's roamed her face, taking in every detail.

"Tell me what has happened. Is it Mother?" He knelt beside her chair and took her hand. She did not resist, but it lay lifeless in his own.

"No. Everyone at Crownhaven is fine. We received the wheat you bought. But I suppose that Carter told you that." Her eyes remained fixed on the fire.

"Why did you not write to me that you were coming? You look very pale. Are you well?"

"Yes, I am fine." She turned her eyes to his at last. "I know you do not want me here."

"Oh, Millie, that is not true. I am so glad to see you. If only you knew . . ." He passionately pressed a kiss on her palm, unable to continue.

"I think I do know. At least . . ." Her brows pulled together in the first expression her face had formed since he saw her sitting there. "I am so confused." The words were barely a whisper.

He tried to draw her into his arms, but she resisted.

"A woman came to see you today." Her gaze returned to the fire.

"Who?"

She looked directly into his eyes. "Angelina La Fleur."

He saw her expression change and knew in a moment that she had seen his guilt. "What did she want?"

"She wants money for the child."

"What child?"

"The child you fathered."

He stared at her in blank horror for a long, silent moment. "She came and told you that?" The clock on the mantel began a grinding whir and struck three. It seemed very loud in the silent house.

"I put her direction on your desk. I am sure that you will do everything that is right by her. Did you buy her that house?"

He dropped her hands and paced to the fireplace. "No," he replied in a hollow voice at last, "someone else did."

"Before you or during? Or did you buy exclusive rights?" she mused. She rose tiredly to her feet. "I should not have come."

"Forgive me, Amelia. It was long ago."

She gave a dry laugh. "There is nothing to forgive. Many men keep mistresses. I would not be surprised to learn that all do. It is quite the done thing. I should hate for you to be *de trop.*"

"No, I gave her up before we were married. I swear, Amelia, it is you I love."

She turned from the door. "I have waited so long to hear that. It is strange that now that you have said it at last, I hate you for it." She leaned against the door-frame. "It does not matter what you say or what is true. Perhaps you did give up Miss La Fleur. Perhaps you have a new lover now. It is your right, and it is of little moment to me. I foolishly thought that I could entice you back to Crownhaven, but I can see now how wrong I was."

He felt the panic rise in his chest. "No! You were not wrong. I wanted to come back. God knows, every day I wanted to go. But the longer I stayed away the more I realized how monstrously I had behaved. When I saw you tonight, my heart . . . I was so happy to see you, Amelia."

"I will go back to Bedfordshire tomorrow."

With two strides, Hunter crossed the room and caught her by the arm. "Stay with me." His voice was low and intense.

"No."

"Amelia, I have been so lost without you. I cannot sleep at night. I have dismissed all the servants. None of our friends know that I am in Town. I spend my days walking and my nights here, staring at the fire. I realized when I saw you that it was you who I was waiting for." He felt a strange relief saying it.

"How romantic," she quipped, attempting to free her arm. "Do not waste your silver tongue on me, Hunter. I am only your wife."

"We will start again. Stay with me."

"I will not."

He took her other arm and held her firmly in front of him. "If you go back to Crownhaven, I will follow you there. I must have you with me."

"What a strange thing to say. Considering that you abandoned me three months ago."

He felt guilt twist sharply in his side. He pulled her toward him, but she resisted, her face turned from him. "I will make it up to you."

"You are only tired and distraught," she said disdainfully. "You now have everything you want, if you would only realize it. You have a mistress and a wife who does not care that you have one. Stay in Town; enjoy yourself.

You can't fool me that this"—she flung off his arm and gestured around the room—"dissipation is a result of heartbreak. It is the result of high living. As long as you do not gamble away all of your fortune, I do not care." She shrugged lightly and gave a brittle laugh.

"Amelia, I love you." He took her face in his hands and forced her to look at him. She was trying so hard to fight off emotion, but he could feel her body shaking as he pressed against it. He had not meant to kiss her, but suddenly he found that he was. He was kissing her with the frantic desperation of a drowning man drawing his last breath of air. She did not move for a moment, but then her arms were around his neck, and she responded with a passion that matched his own.

It was only a moment, perhaps two. He felt her push him away and released her. They stood staring at each other, panting slightly.

"You'll get over it," she spat out. "I got over loving you." He was left standing in the doorway of the study, trying to collect his senses as she stomped upstairs to her room.

Sixteen

She would stay in London. After a long restless night, it seemed a very easy decision to make in the morning. She took a kind of perverse pleasure in knowing that she had turned Hunter's comfortable world upside down with her arrival. He should not be allowed to do as he pleased while she languished alone in the country. It would be preferable to have a miserable existence here, surrounded by diversions, than there, with no company but the dowager's constant complaints and her mother's anxious nagging.

She smoothed her gown over her thickening middle as she dressed herself. No, no one could possibly know yet. She wondered if she should have told Hunter last night. But it would have been all wrong: "Your mistress called to mention that she was expecting. Oh yes, by the way, so am I." She smiled grimly at the thought and sat down to dress her hair. It would be easier to manage once Sarah and the baggage arrived from Crownhaven.

After satisfying herself that her dress was indeed on with the right side out and the front facing forward, she went downstairs. It was early when she descended to the kitchen, but Mrs. Jennings had been working for several hours.

"Hello, milady!" she exclaimed, dusting flour and bits of dough from her hands before she curtsied. "I must say it is nice to have someone else in the house. It was getting very lonely here with just me. Not that I didn't have the men in the stables to look after, but most of the times they kept to themselves." She began crimping the edge of a pigeon pie with a sure hand.

"I would like to hire back the servants. I am undetermined how long I shall stay, but I would like to live in a more conventional manner than Lord Westhaven has been doing." She seated herself on the high stool by the bread board. "I know that you are very busy, but do you think that you can find staff? Or shall I go to the agency?"

Mrs. Jennings beamed and started cutting crusts for tarts with such a flourish that Amelia feared for the woman's safety. "Well, ma'am, I think that some of the old staff have found positions already. I mean to say, Lord Westhaven dismissed them months ago. But I do know that several would come back here in a heartbeat. I also know of several relations of mine that would like very much to be in service." She laughed heartily. "I can whip you up a batch of domestics quicker than I can a meat pie." She gestured at the finished pigeon pie on the sideboard and Amelia was relieved to see that all of her digits were still intact.

"Then I shall leave you to it. If you have any troubles, we can hire people from the agency, or we will send for girls from Crownhaven. I expect that Sarah and my baggage will arrive today, so she can help you." She slid off the stool and left the cook discussing aloud to herself the merits of her various relatives who would like to come up from the country to work in a fine London house.

She next made her way out to the stables, which were considerably more populated than the house. Her coachman, the head groom, and several footmen lounged in the mews smoking their pipes. They immediately knocked them out when they saw the lady of the house approaching. Their guilty expressions suggested that she had been the subject of their discussion.

"Dickson," she addressed the head groom, pretending ignorance of their embarrassment, "is there a horse in the stable suitable for me? I decided not to bring my own mount from Crownhaven."

"Well, milady, I think we do. He's a nice bay gelding. You may try him out if you like and see if he suits you."

"I am certain that he will. My husband has been very busy of late, but we are now preparing to open the house properly. I am certain you will take care of everything." She attempted to look down her nose at him, but suspected that she only looked as though she had a squint. Dickson and the rest of the grooms had the decency to remain sober-faced. Certainly they knew the state of the house and the odd habits of the master.

She went upstairs to change into her habit feeling better than she had in a long time. At least there was plenty to do here. She walked by Hunter's room on the way to her own, but there was no sound from inside. She mentally shook herself for caring where he was or what he was doing. They would live as strangers in a boardinghouse, polite but uninvolved in each other's lives.

"Amelia!"

She reined in the gelding and looked around. Jack flourished his whip over a very dashing pair of matched grays and drove up beside her on the narrow gravel path.

"Jack! What a marvelous high-perch phaeton. I had no idea that you had bought one. Mother will be furious. You will have to do me a great deal of favors in order to keep me from telling her."

"It is grand, isn't it? I have had it only this week. But what are you doing in Town? I had not heard that you were here."

"I only got in last night. Good heavens, the wheels are even picked out in yellow. However did you afford it?"

Jack grinned. "I told you my luck would turn. I am quite rolling in the ready."

"Oh, let me give my horse to my groom to hold, and we shall go for a turn. Do take me up." She dismounted with energy and held out her hand to him while her groom came up and took the gelding.

Jack gave her a hand up and then set the pair off at a spanking trot. "They are something else, are they not? I picked them up from Haversend for a song. I would like to get another pair. Four-in-hand would be quite the thing."

"They are lovely," she gasped. "The perch is exceedingly high, isn't it? I feel as though I am going to be shot into space at any moment. You are sure that you know how to drive such an equipage?"

"Of course, you goose!" He gave another unnecessary crack to the whip and looped the reins so that the horses whisked past a closed carriage with the proper condescension. He allowed his sister to admire his driving skill for nearly the entire route around the park before he remembered his original question. "What are you doing here in town, Milz?"

"Oh, Hunter was still busy on business, so I thought I would join him and amuse myself," she replied airily. "Do mind the woman with the little dog."

"I see her. Well, I say, I am damned glad to see you. It is about time that you came down from the country. It must be dashed flat now that Miriam has gone. Not that it was anything else while she was there. I declare, she must be a changeling. Never a bit of fun in her.

Shall we go another loop?" he asked as they neared the path where Amelia's groom was walking her mount.

"Oh, let's. I am beginning to enjoy the fear that every moment could be my last."

"Fustian. I know very well what I am doing." He gave the whip another flourish to prove this, and Amelia clutched the side of the seat as they lurched into a high speed turn.

"I'm glad to see you, Milz," he said again. "For you see, I have some interesting news. I am going to be married."

"Married? Jack, to who?"

Her brother looked a little sheepish. "Miss Ophelia D'Ore. I am sure you would not know her. I didn't myself until two months ago. I haven't told Mama yet, but she is sure to be pleased."

"Well, of course she will be. Why have you not told her?"

Her brother scowled at the road for a moment. "She is very rich. Sixty thousand pounds in the three percents," he added in a pleading voice.

"Why does that matter? Why should Mama object to that?"

"Dash it all, Millie—it is just that her father is in trade." Jack vented his emotion by passing a landau with something less than two fingers to spare between the wheels. "Well, I know Papa will not mind, but I think that Mama will think that it is not quite the thing."

"Do be careful!" Amelia gave a little shrieking laugh. "Now, Jack"—she tried to recover her breath—"if you love her, no one will mind. Mama will not have the least objection."

"Oh, she is a fine girl." He shrugged.

Amelia stared at him. "You do not sound as though

you do love her. Why ever did you propose? You didn't get into a—a fix?"

"No, no nothing like that. Well, she is a fine girl and . . . well, sixty thousand pounds, Millie!"

"But you have no need for her money!" Amelia exclaimed. "No, let's don't go around again. I feel quite shaken up. Just walk them for a bit."

"You were the one who was always saying that I should marry an heiress."

"Oh, but I didn't—"

"Mean it? Oh, I know. Well, after I saw you last summer while I was at Harrow End dodging the duns, I got to thinking that an heiress might be just the thing." He scratched his chin meditatively with the whip handle. "I got sick to death of home quick enough, what with Miriam squalking all the time, so I decided to take my chances on the marriage mart."

"You are only marrying her for her money? That's infamous!"

Jack had the grace to blush. "She was anxious enough to have me come up to scratch, I should say. She quite set her cap at me. Her family is delighted, needless to say. They would very much like her to marry into a title, you see. Blast it all, Millie, it is the way things always go with marriage."

"I suppose in some ways," she admitted slowly. "But surely there was no need for you to propose to her. Papa would have advanced you some money. He has always done so before."

"Well, I know. But the last time he had to tow me out of the River Tick, he cut up something awful about it, and well, I am not quite sure how it happened that I proposed, but it is done now and there is no getting out of it."

Amelia took his arm. "How terrible. I wish you had not done so. It hardly seems fair to her if you don't care for her except for her sixty thousand pounds. Even if she is getting a title."

"Here is your groom, Millie. I shall set you down. Don't you worry about me. I think that Miss D'Ore hasn't got a heart to break." He saw his sister's anxious expression. "We shall rub along tolerably well," he pronounced cheerfully. "You shall meet her tonight. We are off to the theatre. You will join us, won't you? With Westhaven?"

"I know he would love to go," Amelia replied, resolving to invent a plausible excuse for the doting husband. "You will call for us at seven? I look forward to meeting Miss D'Ore. I am sure that she is a very sweet girl, and I am prepared to love her." She climbed down from the phaeton. "But I do wish that you would tell Mama and Papa."

"I was hoping that you would do it for me. After you meet her of course. You know, tell them that it was a whirlwind thing, love at first sight and all that. You would do it so much better than me."

"I will not." She tried to frown, but could only laugh at his petulant expression.

Suddenly her throat went dry. There she was. That Woman. Angelina La Fleur was walking right there in the park. There was no doubt as to her identity—she was dressed in a fine gold velvet walking dress and wore a set of exquisite amber jewels. Their fine cut very nearly eclipsed the fact that she was somewhat over-dressed for the middle of the day. The ensemble was completed by a small blond poodle and a very well-dressed man.

She felt the air gust out of her lungs when she realized that it was Hunter. Her thoughts in a whirl, she mounted the gelding quickly. She wheeled it away from the woman. "I will see you tonight, Jack. I am off for a gallop to the Serpentine." She fled at full speed before he could reply.

The door to her room burst open with a sound like a shot.

"What do you mean by having your dinner brought up on a tray?" Hunter roared, slamming the door behind him.

Amelia looked up in mild surprise from where she was seated at her dressing table. "Oh, Hunter. I had no idea you were in. I took my dinner up here because I thought you were out. I had no desire to eat on my own in the dining room."

"I am home, and I am going to eat. You will join me." It was barely a question.

"I am sorry. I have already finished. I am in a slight rush, you see. Jack's carriage is waiting for me outside."

"Whose carriage?"

Amelia resisted the urge to cringe and smiled with what she hoped was an infuriating calmness.

"I am going to the theatre with my brother and his fiancée. I would have asked you to accompany us, but I did not know where you were." She picked up a looking glass and examined the back of her hair. "You arrived just in time, Sarah. I should have been lost without you. I was walking around all this morning with half my hair hanging down my back."

Hunter dismissed the maid with a scowl. "I was with Angelina La Fleur," he growled.

"Sir! I can't condone your peccadilloes, and I certainly don't want to hear about them." She gave a false laugh and opened her fan with a flourish.

"She is not with child. Or if she is, she is not very far along. I am sorry to speak so graphically, but you must understand. I ceased my relations with her before we married. She took up with Stanhope shortly afterward. If she is with child, it is not by me."

He was looking at her very intently. She could feel her heart pounding in her temples. The humiliation of knowing that he had had a mistress was salved somewhat. Of course that did not mean he had not replaced the lovely Angelina with someone like her. "You must be mightily relieved," she said lightly, praying he did not note how her voice shook.

"Do you understand what I am saying to you?"

"Of course I do. What is it that you would have me say?"

Hunter's brows drew together. "Say you forgive me. There is no child. We can put this behind us."

"Certainly," she said with a vague shrug.

"The woman only came to call on you because she had seen you arrive and knew that I was from home. In fact, I doubt she had any idea that I was in Town. I have hardly advertised the fact. She was angry that I had discontinued our . . . uh . . . liaison, so when the opportunity presented itself, she concocted the story with the hopes of extorting money from you. She knew I would dispel the myth of her situation soon enough, but I suppose she thought she could squeeze money out of you for a while at least. Perhaps she was just vindictively hoping to drive a wedge between us."

Amelia rose, picked up her reticule, and carefully draped a shawl from her elbows. "But little did she know," she said over her shoulder as she left the room, "we had managed to do that on our own."

Seventeen

Amelia found that her heart was beating hard as she descended the stairs. It had been a rather nerve-wracking interview, but she was pleased. She had not fallen to pieces in front of him. In fact, she hoped she had given a fairly good impression of utter detachment. Oh, but it was painful.

She took one last look in the hall mirror, bared her teeth in a semblance of a smile, and stepped outside to join the theatre party.

"Millie! You are down at last. I was thinking that we would have to come inside and wait for you. You are chronically late in general." Jack jumped out and opened the door for her. "But where is your gallant husband?"

"Oh, dear, it is very unfortunate. He was away from home until two minutes before you arrived. I would have insisted that he come anyway, but he was quite out of sorts." There, that was more or less the truth.

"A shame," Jack replied. "I have not seen him in an age. I was hoping to have to ride on the box, what with you and Hunter inside with Ophelia and her companion. Dash it all, but Hunter certainly has a lot of business to attend to. Do you suppose he has secret dealings with Whitehall? You know, with the war and all?"

"Unfortunately, I don't believe that it is anything as interesting as that."

Miss D'Ore sat in the coach beside a woman so non-descript she must be a companion. Amelia smiled at the women and then looked to her brother for an introduction.

"Oh, yes, well, Amelia, I would like to present to you Miss Ophelia D'Ore. You know, my fiancée."

Amelia shook hands with the young woman. She was passably handsome and dressed in such a remarkably fine style that Amelia felt herself quite in the shade in her amber gown trimmed with sable. Miss D'Ore's black hair was dressed so that it fell in coils on each side of her thin face. Her dark eyes swept over Amelia's person and seemed to take in everything.

"This is my cousin, Miss Chalking. She is my companion." Miss D'Ore indicated her companion with a careless gesture. Miss Chalking acknowledged the introduction and did not say another word.

"How lovely to finally meet you, Lady Westhaven," Miss D'Ore said. "Jack has often spoken fondly of you and of his childhood in Bedfordshire. How quaint everything must be there. I myself would never dream of living outside London. But I am sure you have been to the capital many times before."

"Indeed, no. I was only here for a month before my wedding last summer."

"You did not come out?" Miss D'Ore's face expanded in an expression of horror.

"Mama wanted nothing better, but Millie never would. She had rather stay at home looking maudlin and weeping over her faraway soldier."

"Jack!" Amelia protested, signaling with her eyebrows that he had said quite enough. "I did no such thing. Miss D'Ore, I did not come out because I was already engaged to my husband. We have known each other since childhood."

"Dear me! How extraordinary! I should have thought that you would have at least hoped for a season, just to make certain that the match suited you. I assume that it was something concocted between the two families. My own dear mama and papa had some such a scheme. I had been betrothed to Mr. Winthrop Bell since I was in leading strings. But I will tell you, Lady Westhaven, as soon as I had my own season, I found that I could do a great deal better for myself than the son of a draper. I told my parents that under no condition would I be coerced into a marriage that was now repulsive to every fiber of my being. Yes, indeed. Mama and Papa were quite put out, on account of the fact that they were friends of long standing with his family, but they soon saw that a season amongst the London *ton* had given me hopes for a quality of man much finer."

"That would be me." Jack laughed,

"Indeed." Miss D'Ore patted Jack's arm with a finely gloved hand.

"I am so happy for both of you," Amelia said. "When do you hope to marry?"

"Oh, good heavens, I should think that it will take quite some time to plan the type of wedding that we intend to have. My parents have yet to throw the first betrothal ball. In fact, the announcement has yet to be put in the paper. On account of the fact that your papa is ill."

Jack squashed his sister's toe painfully with his own and shot her a very expressive look.

"Yes, of course. Well, he is much better now," Amelia said through her teeth. How like Jack to make up such a thing just to postpone telling Mama and Papa. She changed her tone and exclaimed, "What play are we to see tonight? I am so looking forward to it."

"Such a remarkable show of enthusiasm, Lady Westhaven," Miss D'Ore tittered. "To look forward to going to the theatre when you do not even know the name of the play. How delightfully ingenuous." Her flat voice grew even more tired as she leaned back against the squabs.

"We are to see *The House in Essex*. I know nothing about it. I fancy it will close within a week," Jack replied.

"Indeed, I think it sounds remarkably dull. My family owns a house in Essex. We are hardly ever there, it is so very dull. I would prefer to live in London for the rest of my days. I doubt there is a decent modiste for miles around our house there."

Miss D'Ore continued to describe in excruciating detail the various merits of her family's estates, while Jack rolled his eyes in such an obvious manner that Amelia was quite uncomfortable and was forced to refrain from looking at him. Her head was fairly pounding by the time they reached the theatre. The building was not nearly as crowded as it had been during the season, she was assured by Miss D'Ore, but it seemed quite full of people who had no compunction about elbowing one in the ribs or treading on the hem of one's gown in their mass push to see and be seen.

Although the crystal chandeliers cast quite a flattering light on everyone, Amelia could not help but notice that some of the ladies present were not exactly Quality.

"Ladies of the Evening," Jack announced, elbowing her and rolling his eyes toward a pair of women wearing the most remarkably low-cut gowns. "They try to keep them outside the theatres, but they will keep coming in."

"Don't be vulgar, Jack," Miss D'Ore said repressively. "Pray do not notice them, Lady Westhaven."

Amelia could not help but look for Miss La Fleur. Thankfully, that particular woman was not present this evening.

As she sat in the box, she was reminded of the last time she had come to the theatre, shortly before her wedding. Hunter had been in good form that night, laughing and teasing her. She scowled and surreptitiously rubbed her temples. It was only because she had the headache that she was out of temper.

Jack took advantage of the fact that Miss D'Ore was conversing with an acquaintance and leaned over the back of his sister's chair. "What do you think of her?"

"She is lovely. Really, Jack, she seems very affable."

"You are a terrible liar, Milz." He smiled grimly. "I find at times that I am quite desperate to end the engagement. She makes my head ache."

"Well, you can't very well call it off yourself. Her family would have your hide. Perhaps you can subtly convince her that you do not suit," Amelia said in an undertone.

"Not likely. The whole family is pleased as punch about the whole thing." He sat down and stretched out his legs as much as the box would allow. "You know, of course, that the family quite concocted the apostrophe. I believe that until this very generation, the family name was D-o-r-e. But once they got rich, it was irresistible not to insert the gentrifying apostrophe. Deh Ore, you know. As in precious metal and gold and things like that."

"How very vulgar you are, Jack," Amelia replied tartly. "Especially when it is the 'ore' you are marrying."

As Jack had predicted, the play was indeed remarkably bad. As they drove home, Amelia mused whether this was the fault of the playwright, the actors, or Hunter. In any case, she had found it hard to concentrate on the ordeals of Countessa Pulvirenti when she had spent the time entire time wondering what her husband was doing.

"My dear Lady Westhaven. How very quiet you are!

Indeed I don't wonder. The play was so dull, you must be positively petrified with boredom. I know what will cheer you up. You shall come to my salon tomorrow night. It is just a little gathering, but I assure you, there will be people there whom you will be happy to call acquaintances when the little season starts. I declare, they are sure to take quite a shine to you. You shall be the toast of the *ton* yet. I have decided that I shall make you fashionable."

Amelia's head jerked around, and she stared blankly at Miss D'Ore. "Indeed," she replied, trying to keep the cool edge from her voice. "How very kind of you."

"Millie doesn't need to be brought into fashion. She is quite happy as she is," Jack announced.

"How vastly diverting you are, Jack," Miss D'Ore replied with a laugh. "I only wish to provide Lady Westhaven with a venue in which to shine. She has been so terribly rusticated in the country." She patted Amelia's hand in a condoling manner.

She and Jack began a long meandering exchange regarding the quality of Amelia's country life. She bid them good night with relief at last and nearly ran up the steps to her own house.

The house was dark and still. Harwell, newly reinstalled as butler, lit her way upstairs without a word. Amelia was forced to admit to herself that the burning feeling racing through her veins was fear. Perhaps Hunter was waiting up for her and would scold her for her rude behavior this evening. Perhaps he would send her back to Crownhaven. Perhaps he did not care at all and had gone peacefully to bed.

They passed his door and she could see that the rooms were still lit. She resisted the urge to tiptoe. But there was no sound as she passed, so she thanked the butler and dismissed him at the door to her chambers. She rang for Sarah and sat down at her dressing table, reminding herself that it was not at all necessary to make sure that Hunter had not fallen asleep with the candles burning dangerously near his bed curtains.

Sarah entered, cheerful and full of chat. She insisted on being told the plot of the play while she brushed out her mistress's hair and helped her into her nightrail. Her enthusiasm was infectious, and Amelia felt much better as she fell asleep, unaware that the candles in her husband's room remained lit for many more hours that night.

"Lady Westhaven, you are the cruelest of women," Lord Derry drawled into her ear. "How can you look at me with those eyes the green of the Aegean Sea and tell me that your husband would be furious?" His hand tightened around her fingers.

Amelia tried to concentrate on the minuet and not on his encroaching fingers. "But he would. I am afraid that I cannot allow you to take such liberties." She smiled politely. "Although a drive out to Wimbledon does sound lovely, even if I took a companion, it would not be proper to go with you."

"Ah, but my dear, you wound me. You use this husband of yours to put me off, when you know that if you wanted to, you could indeed drive out with me tomorrow. Lord Westhaven never escorts you to these parties. He is in his own world. Let him fight his own battles in his head. He is like Don Quixote and his tilted windmills. He likely does not know nor care what you do with your time . . . or affection." He looked intently into her eyes.

She turned her head and gritted her teeth. Was this man impervious to hints? "I believe that Don Quixote tilted *at* windmills. The windmills themselves were likely quite upright. If you are implying that Lord Westhaven is soft in the head, you are absolutely wrong. My husband is very busy. He would like to escort me to these events, but he is involved right now in taking his seat in the Lords. He would be very irritated if he thought you were pursuing an improper sort of relationship with me." She looked up at him frankly. "And so would I."

Lord Derry bridled. "Indeed." His brows rose in sarcastic arcs. "I had no idea you were so prudish, Lady Westhaven. How very countrified. They must have very odd notions of amusement in Little Hissings. Perhaps I should count myself lucky that you are allowed to speak to gentlemen at all." He bowed over her hand with the barest civility and left her by Miss D'Ore's side.

"Oh, dear," that woman remarked, watching Derry's stiff back disappear into the crowd. "What have you done to offend him, Lady Westhaven?"

"It was nothing." Amelia willed the angry flush to leave her cheeks and tried to assume a neutral expression.

"Well, don't mind him. I know him very well, and he is easily annoyed. Of course I have never faced his wrath myself. In fact, I believe he has said that I am charming. But indeed, you must pay him no mind." She adjusted her elegant evening toque slightly. "What a sad crush this is. When I am married I am sure that I will not try to cram this many people into one room without a single open window. The ballroom is far too small by any account. There is barely enough room for forty couples to stand up. How big is the ballroom at Harrow House here in Town?"

"Indeed, I hardly know. Something like this one, if I recall."

"Well, it will have to do. I am certain that we could refurbish it quite nicely. Perhaps another room can be knocked into it to make it bigger. How big is the ballroom at Harrow End in Bedfordshire?"

Amelia swallowed her annoyance. "It is bigger than

this. It is really a nice room. I am certain that it will suit you."

"You will have to draw me a diagram of the entire house. I do so enjoy thinking of the changes I will make there when I am married. Jack is being quite naughty and refuses to show me the town house. Perhaps he wishes to surprise me, but I do wish I had a good idea of what the drawing rooms look like. I could get a much better idea of the kinds of routs I can hold there if I see it."

Amelia forced herself to draw a deep breath before she replied something noncommittal. Her head was beginning to ache.

"I wonder, Miss D'Ore, if I might ask your coachman to take me home. It is not far, and he will be back long before you are ready to leave."

"Why Lady Westhaven, are you ill? The evening has hardly begun."

"No, I am only tired."

"I must protest! You are always tired! You have said that you are tired at every ball in the last two weeks. You hardly even stand up to dance with anyone and yet you are tired. I must have Dr. Silow call upon you. He is the most fashionable doctor in town. He has no time for new patients, but I will prevail upon him to see you." Miss D'Ore patted her hand. "You do look rather peaked. I would recommend Brighton for a sea cure, but it is such a terribly unpleasant time to go. There is simply no one of fashion there at all now." She took Amelia forcefully by the elbow and led her toward the entrance.

"Perhaps I should take leave of Jack and our hostess."

"Oh, don't bother with Jack. He is off in the smelly card room, playing faro, smoking, and losing my dowry," she replied scornfully. "You may take leave of Lady Hampstead on your way out."

Eighteen

Amelia pulled herself up the stairs. Everything about her ached. Perhaps she should see a doctor. But there was nothing really wrong with her. Only that she was with child and was keeping too many late nights.

The experience with Lord Derry had been humiliating. How dared he take such liberties! She closed the door of her room behind her and began plucking pins from her hair. No wonder he had gotten the wrong idea. She had been seen about Town for weeks now and never in the company of her husband. It would be generally assumed that they were living separate lives and that she was available for liaisons.

Her fingers stilled. Something must be done. Before she could change her mind, she went quickly to the door that connected her rooms with Hunter's. She could see that his room was lit. At least he had stopped sleeping in the study these days. There was no answer to her knock.

She pushed the door open and found the room empty. The fire was neatly banked against his arrival and his dressing gown and nightshirt were laid on his bed. The clock on the mantel showed it to be near eleven. It was still early. She looked about the room. It was strange; she had never been in this room. Even on their wedding night, that awful night in this very house, he had come to her chambers.

It was a nice room, very plain, with sober green drapes and gold and green wall hangings. She trailed her fingers along the counterpane as she walked around the bed. No, there was really nothing here that was very Hunterish. She picked up a sliver of shaving soap and sniffed. That did indeed smell of him. She inhaled deeply.

"What are you doing?" came a voice from the doorway.

Amelia spun around, tucking the soap behind her back like a guilty child. "Hunter!"

"Why are you in my room?" He approached her and reached around her to see what she held. This brought him very close to her indeed. She felt the hair on her arms stand on end.

"I was waiting for you," she replied, willing the flush to leave her cheeks.

"Smelling my soap?" He looked at it, sniffed, and then laughed at her.

Her heart began a disobedient tattoo. It had been so long since she had seen him laugh. "I wanted to speak with you. Where have you been?" She felt a frisson of fear as soon as the words left her mouth. It was not likely that she would be pleased with his answer.

"I was at Boodles. I walked home." He shrugged lightly. The laughter had died out of his eyes. "Where were you?"

"The Hampstead Ball." Her words came out a little shaky. He was still standing far too close.

"You are home very early." He moved away, toying with the cake of soap he still held. Amelia felt as though she could finally draw her breath again. "Was it not the sad crush you had hoped it would be? Was Jack's fiancée tired at last of flaunting her newfound respectability at every party she can manage to be invited to?" His back was to her as he faced the curtained window.

Amelia scowled. "How terribly elitist of you. She is a fine woman and has been very kind to me," she announced, momentarily forgetting that half an hour before she had been thinking much unkinder thoughts about the woman in question.

"Miss D'Ore cannot help that she is a tradesman's daughter and Jack cannot help it that he proposed to her. Well," she recanted in an altered tone, "I suppose he should never have done so, and he did it for all the wrong reasons, and I suppose he could stop gambling, but that is not the point. They have contracted an alliance based on their needs, and it seems very sensible."

"Much more sensible than marrying for love. Is that what you mean?" Hunter's dark eyes were dangerously shuttered.

"No," she replied, tartly. "I merely meant that they are each getting what they want from the marriage." She felt her pulse begin to pound heavily and her limbs take on the jingling tingles reminiscent of having taken too much tea. She supported herself with a hand on the bedpost, knowing that she was treading on dangerous ground.

He crossed the room to her in two strides. "What is it that you want?" he demanded, his voice softly veiling the edge to his words.

Amelia clenched the bedpost tighter. How dared her body betray her like this! It was poisoning her mind with extremely distracting thoughts. She fixed her eyes on his cravat.

"I can no longer go to these *ton* parties alone," she announced, aware that her voice had a shameful quaver to it.

"We will hire a companion for you, if you feel as though the presence of Miss D'Ore is not sufficient. I am surprised, as it is *you* who is supposed to be lending *her* countenance, since you are the married lady."

"I don't want a companion." There really did seem to be something wrong with her voice. It kept coming out all strangled and breathless.

"Yes, yes, that might constrain things. You must be enjoying your newfound freedom as a married lady. No doubt the *ton* has been regaled with harrowing tales of how your husband kept you locked in a tower in Bedfordshire while he was living the high life in Town." He did not touch her, but he was so close that she could see her own quick breath fluttering his neckcloth.

"How dare you!" She stepped away so that she could look up to his face. "I have never said a word about you." She could not keep her eyes upon him, his expression was so intense. She flung herself away from him and began to pace the room with her arms folded hostilely. "I need you to escort me."

"Why?" he drawled out, leaning against the bedpost she had vacated.

"People are beginning to note that we do not go about together in company. Gentlemen are beginning to think that I am"—she deepened her scowl as she felt the color rise in her face—"available to take a lover." She spat the words out quickly and turned on him with her chin raised pugnaciously.

"Indeed?" he replied, in that same bored tone. "Well, I am not stopping you. I supposed it was the least you would do after your discoveries of my past indiscretion. I had suspected Miss La Fleur's improvident announcement, however untrue, forfeited my right even to have an heir by you first. I fully expected you to try to pawn off someone else's brat as my own."

She had listened to him in dumbstruck horror, but now she fell upon him with murderous intent. The struggle was a brief tangle of fists, knees, and elbows, but in a moment Hunter had entrapped her wrists in his hands and had her body pressed between himself and the end of the bed. They stood for a moment, panting, their eyes locked in unveiled, mutual hatred. A streak of blood slowly welled up along his cheek.

"You are bleeding," she announced at last.

"I deserve to be. I should be called out for having said that."

"Yes, you should."

"I didn't mean it."

She could not respond. Her throat felt as though it had closed off entirely. His body was still pressed the length of her own.

"Amelia." His voice was low. He dropped her wrists and took her face between his hands.

She had dropped her eyes to his chin, but now made the mistake of looking into his eyes. His lashes were so long, they were even tangled at the corners.

"You know I did not mean that. I have no doubts as to your fidelity."

"Please let me go." She felt a blush heat her face when she realized how unconvincing she sounded.

"Not until you say you forgive me," he replied, his fingers moving slightly against her jaw.

She wondered vaguely if his eyes were made up of only pupil. "Yes, yes. Now let me go." She was suddenly aware that the slight swell of her belly was pressed against him. This was definitely not the time for him to notice that she was with child.

"But you must hear me out first." Hunter's hands had unconsciously wandered down her neck and were exploring the curves of her back. "I would be honored if you wish to have my company. I know that I have not been very . . . amusing of late." He frowned.

Amelia's bones went tallow soft. "No, you haven't," she managed in a whisper. "Let me go, if you please."

She tried to hold her breath so that her middle didn't bulge. If it wasn't for that . . . she shuddered to think what might happen. Every resolution she had made over the last month was melting beneath his touch. She saw the look of hurt cross his face and his arms dropped to his sides. She felt suddenly cold where his hands had been.

She longed to throw herself at him and explain, beg him to share her joy in the coming child. But not now. Not after she had stayed silent for so long. Not after what he had said tonight. A voice in her head asked pointedly when *would* be a good time, but she clasped her hands tightly in front of her and turned to walk the length of the room to put some space between them.

"You have changed so much," he said. His brows drew together, not in his usual expression of frustrated annoyance, but in puzzlement.

"I suppose I have."

"I hardly know you." He watched her pace the length of the room again.

"I don't believe you took the time to know me," she snapped, her thoughts coming back into focus now that he was no longer holding her.

"You are right." His voice was low. "I have so much to explain to you. There was so much that I had to do before I could get back to the business of living."

"Then explain. How nice it would be to know that it was something other than loathing for your new wife that made you hie back to Town after less than two months with her."

Again he looked stung. "Is that what you thought?"

"What else could I have thought, Hunter?" she asked impatiently. "You told me that you married me because you pitied me. What else would you have me think?"

She was not about to shout, but her voice dropped to a dangerous hiss.

He crossed the room to her in two steps and grasped her by the forearms. "But I was wrong. It was me. I hated myself so much that I hated you for loving me. It all makes sense to me now."

"Indeed," she said through a clenched jaw. "How marvelous that everything has been resolved in the blink of an eye." She wished he would not stand so close.

"Well, it has not been easy," he replied with an offended look.

"I don't know what you are talking about."

"I can't explain. I wish I could. For reasons of . . . other people's privacy, I cannot really explain, but you must understand that my leaving had nothing to do with you. I had personal business to take care of."

Amelia looked at him with an expression of patent disbelief. "Of course. Business." She tried to ignore all the possibilities that raced through her head. Was he supporting a secret wife and family? Did he have trouble with the law?

He took both of her hands in his and held them tightly. "I have been an idiot. Even just tonight I have been an idiot. Forgive me for all the things I have said. Please say that I have not lost you. I will make you learn to love me again."

This could not be happening. The words she had been longing for months to hear whipped her mind into a frenzy of fear. She was just beginning to know that she could live without him. She was just getting over the heartbreak of his rejection. How could he now turn to her with such pleading dark eyes and announce that he wished for her love? No. She could not give it away again and risk everything she had worked so hard to build for herself.

"Let's not talk such nonsense. All I asked was for you to accompany me in the evenings on occasion." She smiled in what she hoped was a polite and firm manner, disengaged her hands, and fled the room.

It was only by clenching the back of the brocade wing back chair before the fire that he kept himself from pursuing her. The irony of the situation made him feel like breaking the chair to matchwood against the hearth. Now he was ready. He had buried his ghosts and was ready to start his life again.

And now she had given up. He would have given anything to see that worshipful adoration in her eyes that he had seen when they were first reunited. He recalled how distasteful he had found it and wished very much that he could smash that other self in the mouth.

He rang the bell for his reinstated valet and took off his coat. It had taken enough rejection to alienate her. It would take a lot more wooing to get her back. He smirked at himself in the glass.

"Major Romeo," he mocked the reflection with a twisted smile.

The valet entered the room and looked bewildered to find his master laughing out loud in an empty room.

"Ah, Caldwell, sound the battle cry. Tomorrow we lay siege."

Amelia was deep in a fascinating conversation with the housekeeper regarding household linens when Harwell gave a delicate cough from the doorway of the linen closet.

"A Mrs. McGloin has called for Lord Westhaven, your ladyship. I informed her that he is out, and she says that she would like to speak to you. I have put her in the second-best salon."

"Why the second best? Who is she?"

"I am sure that I do not know, your ladyship."

Another strange woman come to call on her husband? She marched down the stairs with a grim expression. At least this one was married. Or pretending to be. Perhaps Miss La Fleur had married and changed her name. She entered the room, half-expecting to see Hunter's former mistress and found a complete stranger.

She was dressed neatly, if somewhat plainly, and was definitely of the age to have been one of Hunter's schoolteachers rather than a mistress.

"Lady Westhaven," the woman said, as she rose to her feet. "How kind of you to see me. Forgive me for intruding on you when we have not met. I am Mrs. McGloin."

"How do you do?" Amelia shook the woman's hand, feeling at a loss for what to say. She had never seen her before in her life. To cover her confusion, she rang for tea.

"Do you not know who I am? Did the Major not tell you what he did for my family?" Mrs. McGloin looked taken aback. "But of course he would not. What a wonderful, kind, thoughtful man." She pressed her netted mittens against her heart and gave a gusty sigh.

Amelia wondered if this woman could possibly have entered the wrong house by mistake.

"I came here today to bring a little something for the major. To show him our eternal gratefulness for what he has done for us and what he did for poor dear Richard." She produced a basket from behind her unfashionably voluminous skirts. "See, I have brought you some calvesfoot jelly from my sister in Kent. I daresay you must have as much trouble as we do getting it here in London. Hers is very good, I assure you. Gerald made him a very clever shoehorn, and I embroidered some slippers." She put these articles on the table in a little pile. "I know that they must seem like nothings to you, Lady Westhaven, but we wanted to do something in our little way to thank him." She blinked very hard for a moment.

"Madam, you are so very generous. I am certain that my husband will be deeply touched by your gifts. But I must tell you that I still do not understand how you came to be acquainted with him." Amelia picked up one of the slippers and admired it. The workmanship was much finer than anything she herself would have had the patience to do.

"Why Lady Westhaven, my son was in his regiment. He was killed in the battle of Ciudad-Rodrigo." She spoke calmly, but the hand that took up the teaspoon shook a little.

"I am very sorry." Amelia could not think of anything else appropriate to say, so she waited in silence while the woman prepared her cup of tea.

"Just last week the major came to find me. I must say it must have been difficult, as Gerald and I have recently moved to another lodging. Gerald is my youngest son. My only one now. Their father . . . well, we are not certain what became of their father." Her chin tilted up slightly, daring Amelia to comment.

"Why did Westhaven come to you?"

"Why, to tell me about my boy," Mrs. McGloin replied, looking at Amelia as though she was slow. "He came out to our lodgings and sat for a full hour telling me about dear Richard. He was very patient, for I daresay I asked dozens of questions—what was Spain like, what did he do on the day of the battle, what . . . happened?" She drew a shaking breath. "We only received a letter saying that he had been killed. Nothing else. It was so very, very incomplete." The woman cleared her throat self-consciously.

"The major told us everything he could remember," she continued. "It was so comforting. We could not afford to bring Richard's . . . well, to bring him back, you know, so it was the only way that we could finish mourning for him." She stirred her tea and pursed her lips in silence for a long moment.

"I am glad that he did that." Amelia's throat felt very tight.

Mrs. McGloin looked up at last, her eyes shining. "You will never know how much it meant to me. I feel like I can finally grieve properly. He is a great man, the major; I wanted to thank him." She pulled out a serviceable handkerchief and rubbed her nose vigorously.

"Please wait for him. I know he will be back soon. I will send someone to his club to see if he is there. You have brought such lovely things; I know he will want to thank you in person." She rang the bell and requested that a footman search Boodle's. When Harwell left the room, she turned back to Mrs. McGloin.

"You have done more for Lord Westhaven than you can know. You have helped him let go of his past a little. He has suffered so much guilt because he survived the war while so many, like Richard, did not. And I could not understand why he had to come back to London. . . ."

The woman looked at her in astonishment. "It was not only me that he came to see, your ladyship. He has been to see the families of all the men in the company who were killed. There were twenty-five lost in the company of sixty."

Amelia felt her face grow warm with shame. It was terrible of Hunter not to have told her, but somehow she felt as though she should have known. Something inside her began to ache rather painfully.

"Mrs. McGloin, I am so glad you came today." She pressed the woman's thin hand fervently and tried to pretend that she was not crying.

She realized that the woman had been patting her hand comfortingly for a moment, when there was a familiar footstep in the hall. Harwell ushered Hunter into the room.

Amelia sprang to her feet and half-averted her face as she swiped at it with a tea napkin. Her companion gave a cry of joy and began babbling incoherent words of praise and thanks. Hunter looked nonplussed for a moment but then graciously crossed the room to greet Mrs. McGloin.

"Hello, Amelia." He turned to her and bowed over her own hand, holding it for rather longer than necessary. She clutched the hand to her bosom when he released it.

"I will let you converse with your visitor in private," she managed to stammer, unable to meet his eyes. She forced herself not to run as she left the room.

Nineteen

Amelia paced her bedchambers like an animal. In the course of half an hour, the tables had been entirely turned. Her neglectful, brooding husband was suddenly revealed to be everything thoughtful. She looked at the watch pinned to her gown. It was too early to dress for dinner. She desperately needed something to do.

She gave a violent yank to the bellpull and continued pacing. Oh, there was no doubt that everything Mrs. McGloin said was true, and it certainly did explain Hunter's peculiar "business," but she still felt angry. Perhaps not angry, only confused. Why were his doings such a secret? Knowing that he was popping about London doing good deeds did little to salve her hurt at being abandoned at Crownhaven for months.

"Get your bonnet, Sarah. We are going out for a walk."

Sarah's brows rose very high on her freckled forehead, but she did not object. Her eyebrows rose further when Amelia suggested tersely that they exit through the back of the house. Once outside in the last of the bright December sun, with the wind stinging some feeling back into her cheeks, she felt better.

"Your ladyship!" Sarah panted at last. "Won't you please slow down! I can't walk so fast as you, and I am well near to having an attack."

"Oh, dear, I am so very sorry. I was not paying attention." She slowed her strides to a more ladylike pace.

"Is everything all right, ma'am?"

"Yes, yes, quite all right. I just need some time to think."

"Well, ma'am, you had better do your thinking quickly. The sun sets early these days."

"Yes, yes." Amelia suppressed her irritation. She needed to think, but her mind was so jumbled. If only she could be rational about all of this. She very much would have liked to have picked up her skirts and gone for a nice, exhausting run down to the end of the hedgerow and back. But of course that would not do at all. After a few more minutes, during which she realized her pace was again increasing, she turned at last toward home, no more clear in her thoughts than she had been when she set out.

"Milady," Sarah gasped, trotting behind her, "if you ever wish to do this again, you must take Lizzy or one of the other girls. I find it very uncomfortable."

Amelia stopped and held out her hands to the girl. "Forgive me. I will not do this to you again. But, my dear, you must take some exercise or you will grow too weak to climb the stairs, and how will you ever go to visit that handsome footman next door?"

Sarah's reddened cheeks grew slightly more rosy. "I fancy he'll just have to come to me," she replied saucily.

Amelia could not help but laugh and insisted on hearing the story of the romance on the way home. She was still laughing on the way upstairs to change for dinner.

"Ah, Amelia, I am glad to have found you. I wish to speak to you for a moment." Hunter descended the stairs to meet her halfway. He looked perfectly serene.

Amelia gripped the banister and scowled at Sarah who had abandoned her instantly and scampered up the stairs without pausing to catch her breath. She turned to Hunter. "What about?" It was very hard to meet his eyes.

"I was not certain where we were going tonight."

She dropped her gaze to his neckcloth, wishing very hard that she had managed to sort out her feelings.

"I . . . ah . . . that is, I was planning to go to the opera with Jack and Miss D'Ore."

Hunter checked his watch. "Excellent. We shall have time for a little dinner before we go."

"You will accompany me?" she asked in surprise.

"I thought we had discussed this last night."

His tone was completely affable. He obviously had decided to ignore the fact that the discussion of last night had involved her attempting him bodily harm.

"Yes, well, yes, of course. I would be delighted if you wish to accompany me.

He took another step down the stairs, and Amelia pressed back tighter against the banister.

He took her nerveless hand and bowed over it. "I will see you at dinner then." He smiled and lightly descended the stairs.

Amelia was glad he did not look back. His smile had exhausted any willpower she had left. She clung to the banister for a moment, trying to marshal her wits together. It was not fair. She had worked so hard to be free of him.

She pulled herself up the stairs, irritated that her legs still felt trembly, and found Sarah in her chambers virtuously laying out evening clothes.

"I have half a mind to discharge you, Sarah. How could you abandon me like that?" she laughed.

"I am sorry, ma'am. But, well, I thought he might wish to speak to you alone." The maid ducked her head sheepishly and conscientiously smoothed the fringe of the India shawl she was holding.

Amelia sniffed dramatically and then stepped over to

the dresses lying on the bed. "Oh, dear, these will not do at all. Do I own nothing flattering?"

"But you picked all of these gowns yourself!"

"I must have been out of my mind. Besides, I need to start being more careful what I wear."

"Have you told him, milady?"

Amelia looked at her in surprise. "No. But I see that I did not have to tell you."

The maid's cheeks went red. "It is just beginning to become obvious. But it is impossible that I should not know. I see you undressed every day." She turned to pick up several of the offending gowns. "But he hasn't seen you undressed in—"

"Enough, Sarah!" Amelia could not help laughing through her shame. "Do not remind me that nothing is secret in this house. You are an impertinent baggage."

Sarah nodded cheerfully and went upstairs to search out another dress.

Amelia sat down at the dressing table. It seemed that everyone in the household knew she was with child except Hunter. She should have told him long ago. Now it seemed that the longer she put it off, the more awful it would be. Of course the secret could hardly keep much longer.

"Tonight," she promised her reflection. "No matter what."

Sarah returned from her foraging with a gown of Lincoln green silk trimmed with gold rouleau. It had never been Amelia's favorite, but tonight, when she held the fabric against her, it brought some color to her pale cheeks.

"This one will be fine." She pinched her cheeks while Sarah tied the tapes of the dress.

She felt foolish as she revolved slowly in front of the mirror after the maid had done her hair. Why was she so nervous? Hunter had seen her a thousand times. It could hardly matter what she looked like tonight. Only the thought of being rudely late to dinner propelled her downstairs and into the drawing room.

Hunter's smile when she entered made her insides perform the same uncomfortable trick that they had done on the stairs. He looked revoltingly relaxed and charming.

"How beautiful you look, Millie." He took her hand and examined her with exaggerated minuteness. "What a shame that you are missing something."

"I don't understand what you mean."

He produced a small jeweler's box. "This. I think that this will complete the picture."

She hesitantly took the box from him. Inside lay a set of emeralds beautifully set in delicate gold filigree. She could only blink at them in surprised admiration.

Hunter leaned over and looked up into her face. "To match your eyes," he said, his own twinkling. "I recall quite clearly now that they are not blue at all."

"They are lovely. But there was no need for you to—"

"Oh, but there was. What use do you have for sapphires when your eyes are not blue? We shall have to return those."

Amelia gave him a mock frown. "We shall not." She removed the pearls she had chosen to wear with the dress and put on the emeralds.

Hunter moved behind her to fasten the clasp. "How fortunate that you wore green tonight." She could feel his breath on the back of her neck. Every hair beneath his fingers stood on end.

"Indeed." The word came out a breathy squeak. She turned to him. "Thank you. It is the most thoughtful thing you have ever done for me."

He took her by the shoulders as if to make her pay attention to what he said. It had the unfortunate opposite effect. She could pay attention to nothing but his closeness. "And that is a terrible thing," he said softly. "I hope to rectify it over the next fifty years."

Amelia hardly heard him. She tried to drag her eyes from his mouth. "Thank you," she repeated weakly.

"You must thank me in another way." His arm went around her waist and he closed the space between them.

She felt a frisson of panic. "Please, no, please. I am not ready. Don't make me fall in love with you again." She tore herself out of his arms and fled to the window.

"Amelia." His voice was pleading

"Don't," she insisted, hating the weak sob in her throat.

"Dinner." Harwell entered and intoned the word as though each syllable contained unnamable nuances.

Amelia gave a startled little laugh and allowed Hunter to lead her in to dinner.

Unfortunately, any nuances in that meal were lost on her. Her stomach felt stuffed with cotton wool and everything she ate was tasteless. Hunter seemed just as disinclined to eat, so they both pushed the food around on their plates in a pointless little pantomime.

"I suppose we should go to the theatre. I took the liberty of sending round a note to Jack telling him that he should not collect you, since there should not be room for the both of us in his carriage with himself, Miss D'Ore and her companion." Hunter indicated to a footman to take away his plate.

"I am glad you thought of that," Amelia said as she rose.

"I do not wish to take port tonight. Shall I call for the carriage?" He stood but did not take her arm as he escorted her out of the room.

"Yes, do." She felt a peculiar twitch in her womb that

reminded her of her promise. Not now. Surely there would be a better time.

"Lord Westhaven! What a surprise! I have not seen you in months!" Jack leapt to his feet when they entered the box. "I say, you must have been damnably busy. Was it some havey-cavey Whitehall business? Secret spyings on the French?" Jack gave him a conspiratorial wink.

"I am afraid not. But I am finished with my business at last and shall now proceed to devote myself entirely to pleasure," Hunter replied.

"This is my fiancée, Miss Ophelia D'Ore of Barclay Square."

"How very charming to meet you at last Miss D'Ore. My wife has spoken so highly of you."

Amelia resisted the urge to announce that she had never mentioned the woman except in passing. "And this is Miss D'Ore's cousin, Miss Chalking." She indicated Miss D'Ore's companion.

"Yes, milord, this is my cousin. She is from the north. What a treat for her it is to come out to the opera." Miss D'Ore smiled condescendingly at the frightened-looking woman.

"Indeed." Hunter bowed courteously over Miss Chalking's hand as well. "But you are sitting so far over at the side of the box that you cannot possibly see the stage. I think that if we move all of the chairs over slightly, you will have a much better view."

"How good you are to think of it, Lord Westhaven. How very kind of you to think of everyone's comfort." Miss D'Ore obligingly got up and allowed Jack to move her chair several inches. "Not too far, sir, I would like to see something myself. I don't know why you rented this box for the season. It is far too much to the side of the theatre. I can hardly see anything on stage, but can see everything going on backstage. I declare, it quite ruins the illusion when one can see the performers about to make an entrance."

"Will Signora Paoletti be performing tonight?" Amelia interrupted her, seating herself in the chair Hunter held for her.

"Indeed she will. I should not have bothered to come if she was not. I understand that she could not sing for a week with a putrid sore throat, but it was simply unlawful for them to have put up her understudy. I suppose they should have just closed the theatre. There was no point in anyone going to see an understudy." Miss D'Ore raised her opera glasses and surveyed the audience. "I see that absolutely no one who is anyone is here. The news must not have gotten around that the signora is back. Ah, I see that they are at last putting out the lights. I was so humiliated to have arrived early. I generally like to arrive somewhere toward the end of the first act. But Jack insisted on fetching me at an ungodly early hour."

"The traffic is so bad in this area when it gets later," Jack retorted crossly. "I should like to see some of the performance rather than arrive just when it is over."

"The traffic is heavy because it is the proper time to arrive," Miss D'Ore explained with emphasis.

The first act had begun, but the couple continued their quarrel in conversational tones.

"Promise me we shall never sound like them," Hunter murmured.

Amelia gave him a quelling glare, but could not repress a smile. *I will tell him during the interval if we have a moment alone,* she swore to her conscience. It was unfortunate that she had remained so tongue-tied in the carriage. The exchange before dinner had unnerved her. It seemed very hot with so many bodies in the theatre, so she fanned herself, hoping to slow the blood buzzing through her.

She found herself unable to focus on the performance. Miss D'Ore and Jack continued to snipe at each other and, as Miss D'Ore had predicted, people continued to arrive in their boxes long after the performance had begun.

Amelia jumped when Hunter's hand touched hers. He took her fan from her and began to ply it in front of her. "Thank you," she murmured, curls flying about her face. She wished he had not come. It was impossible to concentrate on anything with his warm arm nearly touching hers.

"I don't think her voice is quite repaired yet, do you, Lady Westhaven?" Miss D'Ore asked.

"I think she sounds very well."

"I believe I detect a faint raspiness in her higher register. She is really hardly worth listening to. Perhaps we should consider leaving after the first act. We could go to Lady Cork's ball. I am certain that you must have received an invitation. Did you not?"

"I don't recall." Amelia stared hard at Signora Paoletti, hoping to discourage Miss D'Ore. In the midst of her aria, the singer gestured broadly and her cloak swung out behind her as she turned. The trailing edge of it swept past the footlights, and Amelia saw a curl of smoke.

"She is on fire!" she cried out. The audience gasped in collective horror as the signora realized her peril and ripped the cloak from her shoulders. The last note she sang hung trembling in the air as she flung the cloak from her and took a breath to continue. The audience burst into wild applause at her aplomb.

"Now that is a real performer," Jack shouted.

Amelia felt Hunter go tense beside her. The signora had thrown the burning cloak to the side of the stage, and from their box at the side of the theatre, they could obliquely see stagehands running to put it out. But it had slid too close to the heavy velvet masking curtains, and they were beginning to smolder.

Hunter leapt to his feet, craning to see if the stage hands could control it. The signora continued to sing.

"Dash it all, Hunter, what are you doing? I can't see with you hulking in front of me," Jack protested.

"We will have to leave. They cannot put it out. Stay calm, but leave now. In another moment the audience will see, and there will be a madhouse in here."

"What! What are you talking about? Have they not put out the fire?" Miss D'Ore jumped up and began looking about her wildly.

Hunter jerked Jack from his seat and pushed Miss D'Ore toward the door. "Take the ladies out," he commanded in a voice that brooked no argument.

"Hunter, where are you going?" Amelia struggled to free herself from the hand that Jack laid on her arm.

"Go." He shoved her and Miss Chalking out the door. "I will be right behind you. Stay together and alert the watch if no one has done so."

"Dear God, Lady Westhaven, let us go!" Miss D'Ore shrieked. The rest of the audience was beginning to rumble as the smoke from the burning curtain wafted out into the audience. Jack re-attached himself to Amelia's arm and dragged her out of the box. People were beginning to emerge from their boxes all along the hallway in varying states of panic. Behind them, across the pit, and flowing from box to box was the wave of cries: "Fire!"

Twenty

When they reached the broad stairway, it was already flooded with people. Amelia strained to see Hunter, but the crowd behind them pushed them bodily down the flight. The noise had reached a fever pitch, and the whole area was a jumble of elbows and backs.

Miss D'Ore dug in her heels and stopped the foursome with difficulty. "I must go back. I forgot my wrap," she panted, wild-eyed. "Anne, get my wrap," she commanded Miss Chalkings. The companion was swept away downstream in the current of people. She did not appear to be trying too hard to get back to them. Miss D'Ore shrieked after her for a moment, then turned and tried to claw her way back up the stairs. She was pressed back by the wall of people.

"Don't be a fool!" Jack grabbed her around the waist and dragged her down the stairs.

Amelia watched them being washed away from her as she stood pressed against the sweeping marble rail of the steps. She felt dazed by the shouting around her and not a little afraid that any movement on her part would result in her being forced over the banister. It was a long drop to the marble floor.

Resolving that Hunter would meet them outside and be worried when she did not appear, she allowed herself to be detached from the rail and pushed out the lobby and into the street. The area in front of the theatre was as loud and crowded as the lobby had been. People were shouting for each other, calling for carriages, and in a state of mass hysteria that frightened her almost to immobility. Some audience members were dodging carriages in the street and fleeing from the theatre on foot while others waited irrationally for their carriages to be brought around. Inside the doors, she could see that the main stairway was packed with people. They could not move down because the throng in the lobby had become too dense.

Amelia was pushed to the side as the roiling stampede continued to spew from the doors. There was no sign of Jack, Miss D'Ore, or Miss Chalking. Or Hunter. Surely he would not stay in the theatre. But then again, with his military breeding, he would probably have some stupid notion that he could not leave until everyone was out. Her heart stopped beating. He would much rather die than flee with the rest of the bleating mass.

She flung herself into the crowd and attempted to fight her way back into the building, but was repelled by the sheer volume of people attempting to fight their way out. Bruised and scratched, she stood for a moment, reeling from the repeated impact of a dozen bodies pushing past her. Through the long Palladian windows she could see a woman being trampled by the screaming hoard. Amelia looked around wildly. No, her shawl had been dragged from her long ago. Frustrated, she picked up the skirt of her gown, wrapped it around her fist, and jammed it through the pane of window glass. The glass was thick and heavy, but she continued to beat it with her fist until she had made a jagged opening. With a final kick at the lowest pane, she climbed over the sill and back into the theatre.

There was a peculiar empty backwater in the corners of the room. She stood almost alone by the window while the clot of people grew at the door. The crowd waiting on the stairs screamed at the people at the doorway who screamed at the people outside to make room for them to get out.

Amelia grabbed a dandy in a purple coat. "Go out the window," she commanded. He looked at the window in horror, obviously weighing the cost of his coat with that of his life and then climbed out. Several others saw him and followed suit. Amelia clawed her way past them.

It would be impossible to make it back up the stairs. No one there could move a foot, but they were being pushed viciously from behind by the people trapped at the top. The smell of smoke in the room whipped the audience into even more frantic jostling. She pushed her way along the perimeter of the lobby toward the doors leading into the pit.

She squeezed through the doors and stood pressed against the wall by the rush of fleeing people. Their terrified faces were strangely lit from the blaze at the front of the stage. As she watched, the burning backdrop fell with a crash and a shower of white and yellow sparks. An answering roar went up from the crowd and they surged toward the exit with renewed terror. The heat was becoming unbearable. She could feel it gusting in hot, dry waves as the rest of the set was consumed. Hunter was nowhere to be seen.

Since she had re-entered the building, she had felt nothing but a grim determination, but now she felt a resurgence of panic. It was impossible to think of finding anyone in this crowd. If Hunter was indeed inside the building, saving babies or whatever it was that foolhardy, heroic people did, where would he be?

The fire brigade had broken in a door, pulled in their tank and begun pumping water onto the blaze. She could see their silhouettes in front of the stage. People

were still struggling to get out into the aisles. Several of
the rows of chairs had been pushed over in the exodus.

There was a commotion behind her at the exit. Someone was shouting above the others. "Go back! Go back!
There is a stage door!"

"Hunter!" She flung herself upon the person in front
of her in her attempt to get to him. The entire mass of
people surged with her toward the exit. They were like
a pack of hunting dogs, climbing on top of one another
and howling.

"Go back!" Hunter shouted again. "You will be trampled in the lobby!" Amelia could not see him, but she
knew that he must be blocking the doorway. The crowd
bellowed an enraged protest.

"Go! Go!" She grabbed the man in front of her and
pushed him toward the stage door at the side of the
flaming stage. He pushed her back and swore. Amelia
ran down the center aisle and through a row of seats
to the side aisle. The heat from the front of the stage
was blistering, but at least the stage door was at the side
of the stage away from the fire. She stumbled up the
steps to the stage. The smoke was choking and stung
her eyes, but the stage door was close by.

When she opened it, the fire gave a great roar and
arched back like a huge flaming snake. The men from
the fire brigade shouted at her to close the door, but
instead she blocked it open with a weight used to swing
the backdrops in and out. The night was freezing com-
pared to the heat in the theatre. Amelia gulped in several breaths before she forced herself to go back into
the building.

"This way!" She ran to the edge of the stage and
beckoned. "This is the way out!" Several people detached themselves from the shouting mob at the door
and ran toward the stage. Hunter physically forced the
others down the side aisle toward the stage exit.

With the new air in the room, the fire had raced along the curtain at the top of the stage and was nearing the side with the stage door. Amelia watched it, trying to shield her face from the fierce heat. She pushed more people out the door and waited for Hunter. The fire brigade continued to shout as the draft from the door swept the flames to new heights. This must be done quickly; the fire was already out of control. Hunter came last, only after he had dragged people from the back of the mob in the lobby toward the closer stage exit.

He grabbed Amelia's arm and pulled her with him as he ran up the steps and out the door. She fell to her knees and fought to breathe while he removed the weight that held it open. "That was everyone," he panted. "The rest went out the front."

He pulled her to her feet and supported her around the waist, slowly herding several bewildered audience members around to the front of the building. The mass of people in front of the building stood watching with morbid curiosity as black smoke heaved from the back of the theatre into the night sky, blocking out the light of the stars.

Several other fire brigades had arrived and were pumping water over the walls of the buildings adjacent to the theatre. Hunter and Amelia made their way to the edge of the crowd. Some of them were audience members, pushing through the crowd mewling plaintively like sheep as they tried to find other members of their party. Others were passersby who were just interested in the spectacle of seeing the opera house burn down.

"The men were so angry that the door was open. It made the fire worse." Amelia watched the firemen pumping at their tanks.

"But there was no other way to get everyone out. The crowd in the lobby was hysterical. People were being

trampled." Hunter's face was shadowed in the darkness
of the street.

"Will the whole thing burn?" she asked, wiping the
sweat from her forehead with an unladylike swipe with
the back of her hand.

"Very likely only the stage." Hunter took out his
pocket handkerchief and applied it to her face. "You
have only succeeded in smearing the soot. You look a
fright, my dear."

She looked down at herself. Her Lincoln green gown
was black with soot. A large rent, likely from her fight
with the window, exposed a shocking expanse of petticoat. The entire ensemble was sprinkled rather liberally
with blood from a cut on her forearm. "I do, don't I?"

Hunter removed his neckcloth, re-folded it, and began to bind her wound. "What is this from?"

"The window, I expect. It is hardly bleeding anymore.
There is no need for you to bandage it."

"Allow me to play the hero for a moment longer, my
love."

She looked at him. "You were a hero. I should like
to kill you."

"Why?" He smiled down at her. He had finished tying
her arm, but retained her hand in his own.

"Because then I had to go back in to rescue you. I
knew you would never leave until you had got everyone
out."

"No," he agreed cordially, his arm stealing around
her waist.

"It is quite inconvenient being married to a hero.
You are always going about helping tenants, saving
crops, finding families grieving over their lost sons,
leaping into burning buildings . . . always going about
rescuing people." She gave him a teasing glance.

"And you were the one who rescued me."

"What a foolish thing to say," she laughed.

"Come here," he commanded, enveloping her in a stinking, smoky, glorious embrace. He gave her a lingering kiss that rendered her entirely inarticulate. "Amelia, from the moment I saw your face in the window on the day I returned, I knew that I was loved," he spoke softly into her hair. "I was not ready for it at the time. I did not wish to be rescued from my own little hell. But you rescued me anyway." He kissed her again.

"There you are. Thank God I've found you." It was Jack. "I found your coachman near hysterics. The devil if you both don't look like you've been to hell and back."

"Where is Miss D'Ore? Is everyone all right?" Amelia regretfully disentangled herself from her husband's arms.

"Ah. Miss D'Ore." Jack squinted up at the smoky sky. "Miss D'Ore has decided that we do not suit. She has ended the engagement."

"Oh, dear, I am certain that it was only the stress of the night. Surely tomorrow she will not feel that way. Such a horrible evening would be enough to overset anyone."

Jack laughed loudly. "I certainly hope she does not rescind on her rescission. I am damned glad to be out of the thing."

"Oh. Well, in that case, congratulations," she stammered.

"Are you injured, madam?" the coachman asked, wringing his hands.

"Thank you, John, I am not. We are both quite unhurt."

"You did not look at the fire, did you?"

"Whatever do you mean? I could hardly help it. I am lucky my eyebrows are not singed off."

"But the child! If you looked into it, the child will have a mark on it from the flames."

"What child?" Hunter demanded.

"Nonsense," said Amelia. "Birthmarks are not determined by looking into fires. That is an old wives' tale."

"What child?" Hunter dragged insistently at her arm.

"But the vicar's daughter . . ."

"Pure coincidence. Cook has seven children, and none with the red birthmark, and surely she looks all day into the fire."

"What child?" Hunter turned Amelia to face him.

"Yours."

A look of terror crossed his face. "You are with child?" He held her at arm's length. "You were running about in a burning building and you are with child?"

"Well, Hunter—"

"When are you due to lie in?"

"Not really the thing to speak of in public," Jack coughed politely, indicating the traumatized mob in the street.

"The end of May."

"A child!" he said in wonder.

"And she looked into the fire." The coachman shook his head.

"Really a thing that should be discussed in private," Jack murmured urgently.

"My child." Hunter gave a stunned laugh.

"Well, of course. I know I should have told you earlier. I wanted to every day, but it never seemed to be a good time and things were so very strained between us."

"Why don't I have your coachman get the carriage and you can have this conversation at home?" Jack elbowed Hunter, his eyebrows straining to migrate into his hairline.

"You should never have endangered yourself like

that, Amelia." He pressed her tightly against him in a fierce embrace. Jack excused himself in an undertone and fled with the coachman.

"I did not want our child to be fatherless just because you were engaged in reckless heroics," she laughed against his coat.

He managed to laugh and kiss her at the same time. "Oh, my darling, we shall both have to be much more prudent heroes from now on."

Twenty-one

She hadn't been so tired since the day she had helped take in the crops with the storm coming. "Oof," she exhaled softly as she lowered herself into the hip bath full of warm water. The soot on her hands and arms swirled off in a fascinatingly disgusting gray mist.

"When I think what might have happened, my lady, I nigh on die of fright. What a shock! I daresay we shall have it in all the papers in the morning," Sarah babbled sleepily. "I don't know why you didn't stay there and tell everyone what you had done. Just think! You might have been given an award. Maybe from the King himself. But then, it was mostly the people in the pit you saved," she mused. "Mrs. Jennings says that the best Quality rents boxes. Perhaps the King wouldn't care that you rescued people from the pit. It might have been better if you had tended to the boxes."

"Please go, Sarah. I know you are ready to drop from sleepiness."

"Oh, no, I'm not, ma'am, really," the maid lied, forcing her tired eyes to open wide.

"Go to bed. It must be near on four o'clock. Besides, I want to be alone."

Sarah looked torn. "Are you sure? I can call the doctor. You look very pale."

Amelia gave a tired laugh that came out more of a

croak. "It is only because my skin is finally coming clean. Please, I just want to think, and I can't do it with you yawning every two minutes." She flicked the water off her fingers at the maid. "Shoo." She watched over her shoulder until Sarah had shut the door and then allowed herself to sink lower in the water.

"So baby," she spoke softly to her slightly rounded belly. "You officially have a Papa now." She smiled. "And what a grand Papa he will be. He will take you driving and fishing and swimming at Crownhaven, and if you are a good little Westhavenling, he will teach you to be as bruising a rider as he is. Perhaps he could teach you to draw as well," she mused. "Hopefully you will have his talent and not be completely hopeless like your Mama." Referring to herself as Mama made her throat close up a little. She continued her monologue in a crooning lullaby. "Yes, little one, you will be as brave and noble and generous and caring as your Papa, too; I know you will."

"But not nearly as bullheaded and blind."

"Hunter!" She turned to the door with a splash. "I didn't hear you come in!"

He closed the door silently and came up to the tub. "Military training does come in useful on some occasions."

"Well, then, I suppose I should be glad you didn't charge your horse in here," she replied, awkwardly pulling her knees to her chest.

His brows drew together slightly. "Amelia, don't be embarrassed in front of me. After all"—he drew up a stool behind the tub so that she could not see his face— "I have seen you unclothed many times."

She felt herself blush and turned her attention to scrubbing her arms. "I'm not embarrassed. I just didn't expect you." She felt his hands on her shoulders push her forward away from the edge of the tub. He took the soapy cloth from her nerveless fingers and began washing her back with slow sensuous strokes.

For a long moment there was no sound in the room but the slight sloshing of the water in the tub. "I am glad the child will not be born until May," he said suddenly.

She had been mesmerized by the shine of the candles on the bath water and the soothing motion of his hands. "Why?"

"Because I *have* been bullheaded and blind." He pressed a kiss into the pile of hair she had pinned to the top of her head. "And now I will have a chance to start again before the child comes."

"Why didn't you tell me that you were searching for the families of the men from your regiment?" she asked softly. "I could have helped you."

He sighed and his breath across her neck made her shiver. "I know. I should have. Oh, Millie." His fingers twined into her hair. "You could have helped me so much. I just wanted to keep you and Spain in separate places in my mind. When I left England I cut myself off completely from it. It wasn't exactly that I hoped to die; I just suspected that I would. How could I allow myself to love you, to long to come home to you when I knew I would die?"

He gave a short laugh. "The water is getting cold, my sweet. Give me your hand." He helped her out of the tub and wrapped her carefully in a towel. He took a long time rubbing it over her body and finally helped her into her dressing gown.

He took the branch of candles and led her into her bedroom. "I have let these things eat at me for too long," he said firmly. "I have finally put the ghosts of those who have died to rest. But at what a terrible cost." He sat down on the sofa and pulled her onto his lap. "I will not shut you out again, Millie. In you,

I have everything to live for." He smoothed his hand over her stomach and smiled. "And just think, when the child is born, I will have a bevy of new worries to obsess over."

"I should have told you right away, Hunter. It was very wrong of me." She ducked her head into the hollow of his neck. "But I was so angry that you left me behind at Crownhaven. And then there was that dreadful La Fleur woman."

His arms tightened around her. "Millie, I am so—"

"You might have picked someone who knows better than to wear rubies with pink. Really, darling!" She laughed and then sobered. "Honestly, we started out all wrong. We will be much better, equal partners if we start again and stop holding back so much of ourselves."

"It is a bargain, my love."

She sat up suddenly. "Oh! I forgot! I have a confession. I suppose I had better tell everything if we are going to begin again."

The crease between his brows reappeared. "What?"

"I read your letters to me. The ones that were in your desk. I shouldn't have, I know." She smiled weakly. "But they were very nice."

"The one where I told you that when I went back to Town after that Christmas when you turned sixteen and pretty all at once, I took a lock of hair from your pony's tail because I was afraid to ask for one of your own?"

She giggled. "And the one where you tried to rhyme 'Amelia' with 'Wisteria'?"

He swept her into his arms and deposited her onto the bed. "And the one where I told you how very much I enjoyed that day in the cottage . . ."

"Oh, yes, I do recall that one vaguely. But do remind me."

"I will."

* * *

"Are you quite warm enough?" Hunter asked his wife for the fortieth time.

"Yes, it's marvelous," she replied enthusiastically. "We must never take the closed carriage again. Jack took me for a ride in his high-perch phaeton in the park, and I thought I would be flung into the tree boughs. But you are a much better driver than Jack."

He shot her a mocking frown. "I should hope so. He wrecked that carriage weeks ago!"

"Did he? He didn't mention it. Well, I suppose he wouldn't, since he knew I would scold." She leaned her face into the wind and inhaled. "I think it might snow."

Hunter squinted at the sky. "Perhaps. But we will be home long before that. Ah, Milz, I am glad you wanted to go back to Crownhaven for the holidays. I feel like it has been forever since I have seen the place." He felt the strange warmth of longing come over him. He had been so desperate to leave Crownhaven a few months ago. Now it seemed he couldn't get there quick enough.

"Well, your mother ordered me to bring you home for Christmas. I think she would have boiled me with the pudding if I had come home without you. And you can't imagine that I was going to stay in London when Jack, Miriam, Lord Wells, and the baby will all be at Harrow End for the holidays."

"Christmas," he sighed. "I can't remember how I spent last Christmas. Sitting in a leaky tent with Caldwell trying to figure out how to dry out clothes when there was no firewood to be burned, most likely."

"Well, if you get nostalgic, we can always trek out to Mrs. Griggs' abandoned cottage." She shot him a saucy look from under the rim of her bonnet.

He laughed. "I have a better idea. We will fix the place up again. It can be our own secret lovenest."

"I would like that." Her smile faded. "You know, Hunter, I made a great many changes while you were gone. I know Carter told you about most of them, but I hope that you won't dislike what I have done."

The house rose into sight and he felt a tightness in his chest. When he had come back from Spain it had still felt like his father's house; it had been a place that trapped him into a domesticity that stifled him. Now it was home. "My dearest, it's your house, too. I am very proud of the role you have taken on in managing the estate. I never knew you would turn out to be such a capable and thoughtful landlady."

"I never knew it myself. And I enjoyed it." Hunter stopped the phaeton in front of the house and went round to help her descend. "I wouldn't say that I enjoyed your absence, but I suppose if you had not gone I would have been one of those mistresses who isn't sure where corn comes from and hasn't got a clue as to where the towels are kept."

Wedgeworth raced down the steps. "My lord! My lady! Thank heavens you are here! The dowager!" He paused for breath, looking uncharacteristically harried.

"Is she ill?" Amelia gasped.

"No, she will be here any minute!"

"What?" Hunter waved the groom who held the horses off toward the stables and put an arm around Wedgeworth's shoulders. "Perhaps you had better explain inside."

He cleared his throat and calmed himself. "This morning a note arrived saying that the dowager had taken the liberty of inviting over all of Lady Westhaven's relatives from Harrow End for dinner." In the entryway, he automatically relieved Amelia of her cloak before he continued. "Her note said that she then realized that the Dower House would not do at all and that she could never entertain in such a hovel and that she had

changed her plans and was going to entertain them
here."

"And she is on her way." Hunter smiled. "How very
like my mother. She would have made a marvelous general."

"Does Cook need help?" Amelia asked quickly. "Did
Mrs. Egan air the bedrooms? They might end up staying
overnight you know. Have Sarah run and get her
mother to help with the pastries, and I'll start setting
the table myself just as soon as I change my clothes."

Hunter smiled as he watched his wife take charge of
the situation. He turned her by her shoulders to face
him and untied the ribbons of her bonnet. "You will
have to find someone else to set the table, my sweet.
You will be needed to greet your guests. I see them, or
rather hear them, coming down the drive just now."

Jack's voice, raised in a rather off-key rendition of
"The Holly and the Ivy," could be heard above a chorus
of laughter.

"Merciful heavens! They're here!" she squeaked.
"And me covered in dust from head to toe. You hold
back the hoards while I change my gown. I'll be back
in a wink." He laughed after her as she raced up the
stairs untying the tapes of her gown as she went.

"Hunter!" Lady Harrow descended regally from the
open landau. "What a marvelous surprise! Camilla said
that you were still in Town. Ah, but she meant to surprise us! That is why she sent the note saying that we
should come here rather than the Dower House."

"Something like that." He decided that announcing
that they had just arrived would make them feel unwelcome. He glanced down at his mud-caked boots and
grinned broadly. Oh well. He was shaking hands with
Lord Harrow when a squall drew everyone's attention.
"Is that my niece?" he demanded, coming up to the
landau to hand Miriam down.

"Indeed it is. Hold her a moment while I get down."

"No, wait!" he protested, but a soft bundle was thrust into his arms. The infant's wail stopped momentarily and it stared at him with wise blue eyes. "It likes me," he stated with dumbfounded pride, just before it began howling again.

"It is not an it; it is Evalinda," Amelia said chidingly as she appeared at his elbow. She looked as cool and unruffled as though she had spent hours readying herself for her guests.

"Then you take *Evalinda,*" he suggested.

"No, wait!"

He transferred the baby to her anyway and then leaned over her and peered at the infant's crumpled face as it wailed. His wife looked up at him happily.

"I say, here is the dowager now," Jack called out. "I thought she was in the house, but here she comes up the drive in a gig. And it's Thomas driving! Grand! Quite a house party you are having, Hunter."

"Oh, yes, well, we wouldn't have it any other way," he replied, stifling a smile and exchanging a glance with Amelia.

"But it was the dowager's idea," she amended sweetly. "You know of course that Cook will kill her," she added under her breath.

"Oh, definitely," he murmured. "We shall probably have to serve pig's cheek for dinner."

"I don't believe there is even that in the house. I think we shall have to serve seven removes of bread and cheese."

"My dear Lady Harrow! What are you thinking to let Miriam stand out in the cold like this!" The dowager lady Westhaven hurried up to the crowd that stood on the doorstep. "And is that the baby? It will have the croup by Boxing Day, mark my words. And you, Lord

Wells! You should be ashamed of yourself, letting your family stand out in the elements! Come in the house."

"Yes, please," Amelia said with a calm smile. "Do come into the house."

The dowager pressed her hand to her bosom. "Yes, yes, that is right. Lady Westhaven is the mistress of Crownhaven now. She is the one who should invite you"

"Indeed she is." Hunter shot his mother a remonstrative glance as he ushered the group into the house.

"So," said Lady Harrow, once they were ensconced in the drawing room. "How did you find Town? Are you just back?"

"Yes, just back," Amelia smiled. Hunter saw that she was looking out to where Cook stood in the doorway of the drawing room, frantically waving a shoulder of mutton. "Perfect," she said serenely in answer to the woman's questioning pantomime. "It is perfect to have you all here."

"I do hope that you were not at the opera on the night of the fire," the dowager said.

"I should say we were!" Jack exclaimed before either Hunter or Amelia could reply. "They were both in there dragging people out of the flames! You should have seen it!" He launched into a fascinating and highly inaccurate account of the evening. "I'd say it was an anarchy society plot against Prinny." He shrugged. "I meant to tell you before if you hadn't got so riled about the phaeton." He glowered at his father.

Hunter looked around him and smiled. It wasn't how he had planned it, everyone descending on them the moment they arrived at Crownhaven, but it was perfect. He watched his mother running her fingertips along the carved grooves of the sofa arms and then check her fingers for dust. Thomas was politely distracting Lady Harrow from the row that was brewing between Jack and his father. Lord Wells bounced his baby daughter

on his knee until she vomited on him and they both
roared simultaneously for Miriam. He turned to
Amelia. She kissed her finger and wiggled it at him; he
could see that there were happy tears in her eyes.

"You wouldn't have liked Miss D'Ore at all Papa, so
there is no need to start kicking up dust over that, too,"
Jack explained with a shrug. "It's a good thing for the
fire, or I would have been leg-shackled to that woman."
He gave an elaborate shudder. "And it doesn't signify
anyway, since it wasn't announced in the papers that we
were engaged. I mean, she did screech that the betrothal was off in front of a lot of people, but everyone
was quite distracted by the fire, so I daresay no one
noticed. Then she caught a glimpse of that Friday-faced
companion of hers trying to slink away and actually ran
after her bellowing. Near gave me an attack of nerves
on the spot to know what a close shave I had had. Then
I had to hunt for nearly half an hour to find Amelia
and Hunter. Their coachman was in quite a taking—I
say," he broke off with a sudden thought, "did you
know that Millie is expecting?"

"What! Why did you not tell me?" Amelia's mother
squealed. "How long have you known?"

"I dashed well forgot clean about it. If you hadn't
cut up about the phaeton . . ." Jack muttered.

"You must call Dr. Lightner right away. He attended
all of my lyings-in," his mother announced definitively.

"Oh, no, Dr. Sterling! He is considered the best!"

"Well, in any case, do make sure you drink plenty of
milk. It is very beneficial."

"Dr. Lightner was educated in Paris."

"I want a grandson. I'll need an heir, as I am going
to murder my son Jack here any day."

Amelia looked at Hunter with a helpless smile. "I'm
so glad we came back," she whispered. "They're per-

fectly frightful of course. Are you wishing yourself back in Spain?"

The family was too involved in firing advice at each other to notice that he kissed his wife right in front of them. He laughed softly. "I would not wish myself anywhere else in the world."

Epilogue

Hunter squinted up at the Spanish sun, took off his hat, and wiped his brow. The dry breeze wafted the air like an open oven door and spun the dust behind the open carriage into brown plumes. "Damn, but it's hot," he said unnecessarily.

"I think it's very nice," Amelia replied happily. She tilted away her parasol and squinted up with him. "I feel like a cat sunning itself."

"I want to be a cat!" a shrill voice piped.

"You can't be a cat, Julia. You are just a little girl," her brother announced with all the superiority of his five years.

"You may pretend to be whatever you like, puss, but don't pull your bonnet off. The sun is very strong today and it will burn your nose." Hunter pulled his daughter onto his lap and re-tied the ribbons of her bonnet. "We shall get you a nice dish of cream when we arrive in Fnentes d'Orono."

"Princess der Oh No?" Julia looked pleased. "I want to meet a princess! I want to be the pussy cat under her chair."

David shook his jumping jack solemnly at his little sister. "Fnentes d'Orono is where Papa hid out in the barn for three days when he and some of the other men got separated from their regiment." He turned around in the seat of the landau and peered down the road. "Will we see the actual barn, Papa?"

"I don't know. It is probably gone. That was a long time ago."

"Will we meet the lady who stitched up Captain Gilling's head?" David's bright brown eyes were so very much like his father's. Amelia felt her heart give a little squeeze of happiness.

She laughed and caught onto her son's breeches before he launched himself out of the carriage. "You know Mrs. Gillings, David. We saw them last Easter. Captain Gillings married the lady who stitched up his head, remember?"

"Her?" he said with obvious disappointment. "She didn't look like the daughter of a gorilla."

"Guerrilla," she corrected. "They are very different."

"I have a picture of a gorilla in my book."

"Mama," Julia interrupted from Hunter's lap, "Grandma West'ven said the sun would give me freckles, but I want freckles. Cece Hart has freckles, and I want them, too."

"Uncle Jack said freckles make a girl look like she has some dash." David carefully examined the jumping jack's nose. "A dash of what? A dash of the brown stuff that freckles are made of?"

"But, darling," Amelia explained to her daughter, "some people don't get freckles. I think that you would either turn brown in the sun like your Papa or turn pink like me."

"Grandma Harrow says Papa is as brown as an Indian because he is always out working with the tenants," her son interjected. "She says Evalinda and I are as wild as Indians. I think she thinks about Indians a lot."

"I want to be pink!" Julia squealed delightedly.

"I think you are better off the way you are, my darling." Amelia turned to Hunter. "Is it strange to be here after all this time?" she asked gently.

"A bit. But I wanted you to see it."

"I wanted to see it very much. I want to see the places you talked about. And I wanted you to have some pleasant memories of Spain."

He brushed her cheek with his knuckles. "I am in different circumstances indeed." He paused and thought for a moment. "It is strange to be here," he said at last, his eyes scanning the mountains in the distance. "I am glad to see how much things have improved. It is hard to see the sites where men I knew died, but not so much as I thought it might be. It would be easy to get maudlin if I were on my own."

"When are you ever on your own these days? The children cling to you like limpets." She moved closer to him and leaned against his shoulder. "And I can't get enough of you myself."

"I want to be pink," her daughter repeated stubbornly.

"I don't wish to be alone." He gently removed Julia's fingers from the ribbons of her bonnet and tied the ribbons together once again. "Do you know," he looked over at Amelia suddenly, "that this is our honeymoon?"

She smiled. "I suppose it is."

"Are we there yet?" David sighed and began resignedly disassembling the limbs of the jumping jack.

"It's a little late," Hunter said apologetically. "Nearly six years after our wedding."

"Well, my darling"—Amelia pressed herself closer to her husband—"we have been very busy."

More Zebra Regency Romances

Put a Little Romance in Your Life With
Fern Michaels

__Dear Emily	0-8217-5676-1	$6.99US/$8.50CAN
__Sara's Song	0-8217-5856-X	$6.99US/$8.50CAN
__Wish List	0-8217-5228-6	$6.99US/$7.99CAN
__Vegas Rich	0-8217-5594-3	$6.99US/$8.50CAN
__Vegas Heat	0-8217-5758-X	$6.99US/$8.50CAN
__Vegas Sunrise	1-55817-5983-3	$6.99US/$8.50CAN
__Whitefire	0-8217-5638-9	$6.99US/$8.50CAN

Call toll free **1-888-345-BOOK** to order by phone or use this coupon to order by mail.

Name_____

Address_____

City _____ State _____Zip_____

Please send me the books I have checked above.

I am enclosing $_____

Plus postage and handling* $_____

Sales tax (in New York and Tennessee) $_____

Total amount enclosed $_____

*Add $2.50 for the first book and $.50 for each additional book.

Send check or money order (no cash or CODs) to:

Kensington Publishing Corp., 850 Third Avenue, New York, NY 10022

Prices and Numbers subject to change without notice.

All orders subject to availability.

Check out our website at www.kensingtonbooks.com